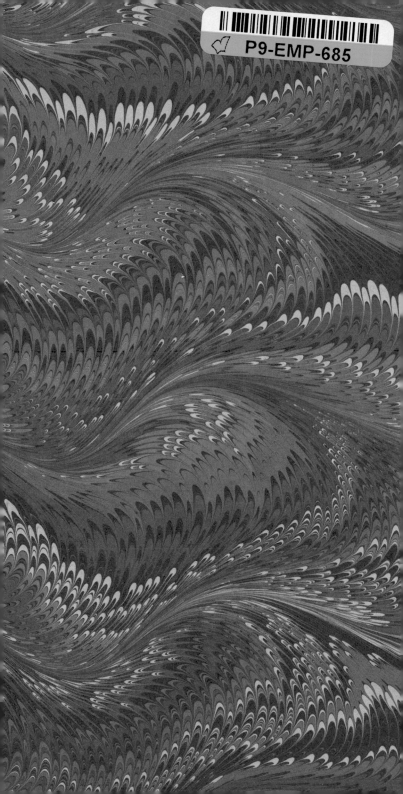

THE
PHANTOM
OF
MANHATTAN

St. Martin's Press
New York

THE
PHANTOM
OF
MANHATTAN

FREDERICK
FORSYTH

THOMAS DUNNE BOOKS.
An imprint of St. Martin's Press.

Library of Congress Cataloging-in-Publication Data
Forsyth, Frederick
The phantom of Manhattan / Frederick Forsyth.
p.   cm.
ISBN 0-312-24656-0 (hardcover)
I.   Title.
PR6056.O699P48   1999   99-15882
823'.914—dc21   CIP

BOOK DESIGN BY CAROL MALCOLM RUSSO/SIGNET M DESIGN, INC.

First Edition: November 1999

10   9   8   7   6   5   4   3   2   1

ACKNOWLEDGMENTS

In attempting to envisage the city of New York in the year 1906 I was given great help by both Professor Kenneth T. Jackson of Columbia University and Mr. Caleb Carr, whose books *The Alienist* and *Angel of Darkness* so vividly bring to life what it must have been like to live in Manhattan around the turn of the century.

For a detailed description of the origins and development of Coney Island and its amusement parks at the same period my thanks are due to Mr. John B. Manbeck, the borough historian of Brooklyn.

For all matters concerning grand opera and most notably the opening of the Manhattan Opera House on December 3, 1906, I had recourse to none other than

ACKNOWLEDGEMENTS

Mr. Frank Johnson, editor of the *Spectator*, who was unstinting in his helpfulness and has surely forgotten more about opera than I shall ever know.

The idea of even attempting to write a sequel to *The Phantom of the Opera* derives from a first conversation with Andrew Lloyd Webber himself. It was during further and intensive discussion that the basic outline emerged between us and I remain grateful for the benefit of his imagination and enthusiasm.

PREFACE

What has now become the legend of the Phantom of the Opera began in the year 1910 in the mind of a French author now almost completely forgotten.

As with Bram Stoker and Dracula, Mary Shelley and Frankenstein, Victor Hugo and Quasimodo, the Hunchback of Notre Dame, Gaston Leroux chanced upon a vague folktale and saw within it the kernel of a truly tragic story. From this he spun his tale. But here the similarities must end.

The other three works became immediate popular successes and remain to this day legends known to every reader, cinema-goer and millions more besides. Around Dracula and Frankenstein entire industries have been built, with scores if not hundreds of reprints and re-creations on film. Leroux, alas, was no Victor Hugo. When his slim little book emerged in 1911 it caused a brief flutter in France and even received newspaper serialization before falling into virtual oblivion. Only a fluke eleven years later, five years before the author's death, brought his story back into prominence and set it on the road to immortality.

That fluke took the form of a very small and genial once-German Jew called Carl Laemmle who had emigrated to America as a boy and by 1922 had become president of Universal Motion Pictures of Hollywood. In that year he took a vacation in Paris. Leroux had by then started to dabble in the smaller French film industry and it was through this connection that the two men met.

In an otherwise desultory conversation the American film mogul mentioned to Leroux how impressed he had been by the vast Paris Opera House, still to this day the biggest in the world. Leroux responded by giving Laemmle a copy of his even-by-then disregarded book of 1911. The president of Universal Pictures read it through in a single night.

It just so happened that Carl Laemmle had both an opportunity and a problem on his mind. The opportunity was his recent discovery of a strange actor called Lon Chaney, a man with a face so mobile that it could assume almost any shape its owner wished. As a vehicle for Chaney, Universal had committed itself to making the first film of Hugo's *Notre Dame de Paris*, then already a classic. Chaney would play the deformed and impressively ugly Quasimodo. The set was already under construction in Hollywood, a huge timber-and-plaster replica of medieval Paris with Notre Dame in the foreground.

Laemmle's problem was what vehicle to offer Chaney next, before he was stolen away by a rival studio. By dawn he thought he had his project. After the hunchback, Chaney would star as the equally disfigured and repulsive but essentially tragic Phantom of the (Paris) Opera. Like all good showmen, Laemmle knew that one way to pack audiences into cinemas was to frighten them out of their socks. The Phantom, he reckoned, ought to do that, and he was right.

He bought the rights, returned to Hollywood and ordered the construction of another set, this time of the Paris Opera House. Because it would have to support a cast of hundreds of extras, the Universal replica of the Opera became the first to be created with steel girders set in concrete. For that reason it was never dismantled, sits on Stage 28 at Universal Studios to this day, and has been reused many times over the years.

Lon Chaney duly starred in (first) *The Hunchback of Notre Dame* and then *The Phantom of the Opera*. Both were great commercial successes and established Chaney as an immortal in that kind of role. But it was the Phantom who so frightened the audiences that women screamed and even fainted, and in a masterly PR coup smelling salts were available free in the foyer!

It was the film rather than Leroux's overlooked and largely forgotten book that caught the imagination of the wider public and created the birth of the Phantom legend. Two years after its premiere Warner Brothers released *The Jazz Singer*, the first talking picture, and the era of silent movies was over.

Since then there have been various representations of the Phantom of the Opera story but in most cases the story was so altered as to be hardly recognizable and they made little impact. In 1943 Universal did a remake of their twenty-year-old property starring Claude Rains as the Phantom and in 1962 Hammer Films of London, specialists in horror movies, tried again, starring Herbert Lom in the title role. A TV version in 1983 with Maximilian Schell succeeded a filmed "rock" version by Brian de Palma in 1974. Then in 1984 a young British director produced a lively but very camp version of the story at a small theater in East London—but as a stage musical. Among those who read the reviews and went to see it was Andrew Lloyd Webber. Unbeknownst to itself, Monsieur Leroux's old story had just reached another turning point in its career.

Lloyd Webber was actually working on something else at the time—the "something else" would turn out to be *Aspects of Love*. But the story of the Phantom stayed in his mind and nine months later in a second-hand bookstore in New York he chanced upon an English translation of the original Leroux work.

Like most perceptions of extreme acuteness, Lloyd

PREFACE

Webber's judgment looks simple enough in hindsight but was destined to change the world's attitude to this ill-used legend. He saw that it was not basically a horror story at all, nor one based on hatred and cruelty, but a truly tragic tale of obsessive but unrequited love between a desperately disfigured self-exile from the human race and a beautiful young opera singer who eventually prefers to give her love to a handsome aristocratic suitor.

So Andrew Lloyd Webber went back to the original story, pared away the unnecessary illogicalities and cruelties featured by Leroux and extracted the true essence of the tragedy. On this foundation he built what, over the twelve years since the curtain first went up, has proved to be the most popular and successful musical of all time. Over 10 million people have now seen his *Phantom of the Opera* onstage, and if there exists a global perception of this story it derives today almost totally from the Lloyd Webber version.

But in order to understand the essential story of what really happened (or is supposed to have happened!) it will be worth spending a few moments examining the original three ingredients out of which the story was born. One of these must be the Paris Opera House itself, a building so amazing even to this day that the Phantom could not have existed in any other theater in the world. The second element is Leroux himself and the third is that slim little volume he churned out in 1911.

The Paris Opera was conceived, like so many other

great enterprises in life, because of a fluke. One evening in January 1858 Napoleon III, Emperor of France,
went with his Empress to the opera in Paris, then sit-
uated in an old building in a narrow street, the rue le
Peletier. Just ten years after a wave of revolution had
swept Europe these were still troubled times, and an
Italian anti-monarchist called Orsini chose that evening to throw three smoking bombs at the royal carriage. They all went off, causing more than a hundred
fifty people to be killed or injured. The Emperor and
Empress, protected by their heavy carriage, emerged
shaken but unhurt and even insisted on attending the
opera. But Napoleon III was not amused and decided
Paris should have a new opera house with, among
other things, a VIP entrance for people like himself,
which could be guarded and remain reasonably bomb-
proof.

The prefect of Paris was the city planner of genius
Baron Haussmann, creator of much of modern Paris,
and he organized an open competition among all of
France's most prominent architects. There were one
hundred and seventy of them who submitted plans, but
the contract went to an imaginative and avant-garde
rising star, Charles Garnier. His project was going to
be truly massive and cost a very large fortune.

The site was chosen (where l'Opéra stands today)
and work began in 1861. Within weeks a major problem occurred. The first diggings revealed an underground stream running right through the area. As fast
as they dug, the holes filled with water. In a more

cost-conscious age they might have moved the project to more suitable ground, but Haussmann wanted his opera house just there and nowhere else. Garnier installed eight giant steam pumps, which thumped away day and night for months to dry out the saturated soil. Then he built two enormous caisson walls round the whole site, filling the gap between with bitumen to impede seepage of water back into the work area. On these massive foundation walls Garnier built his behemoth.

He was successful up to a point. The water was held at bay until he was finished at that level, but then crept back in to form an underground lake beneath the lowest of the layers of cellars.

A visitor even today can descend to these levels (a special permit is needed) and peer through gratings at the buried lake. Every two years the level is lowered so that engineers in flat-bottomed punts can pole around and inspect the foundations for possible damage.

Story by story Garnier's giant rose until he was back at ground level, then went onwards and upwards. In 1870 work came to a halt as yet another revolution swept France, triggered by the short but brutal Franco-Prussian War. Napoleon III was deposed, and died in exile. A new republic was declared but the Prussian army was at the gates of Paris. The French capital starved. The rich ate the elephants and giraffes from the zoo while the poor fricasseed dogs, cats and rats. Paris surrendered and the working class of the city was so enraged at what they had gone through that they rose in revolt.

The insurrectionists called their regime the Commune and themselves the Communards, with one hundred thousand men and cannon spread throughout the city. The civil government had quit in panic and the Civil Guard took over as a military junta, finally crushing the Communards. But during their time in charge the rebels had used the shell of Garnier's building with his labyrinth of cellars and storerooms as a base for weapons, powder . . . and prisoners. Terrible tortures and executions took place in those vaults far belowground and buried skeletons were still being discovered many years later. Even today there is a deep chill there that never goes away. It was this underground world and the idea of a lonely disfigured hermit living down there in the darkness that fascinated Gaston Leroux forty years later and fired his imagination.

By 1872 normality had been restored and Garnier got on with his job. In January 1875, almost seventeen years to the day since Orsini threw his bombs, the opera house, whose conception his act had triggered, held its gala opening.

It covers almost three acres of space, or 118,500 square feet. It is seventeen stories from deepest cellar to pinnacle of roof, but with only ten aboveground and an amazing seven stories underground. Surprisingly, its auditorium is quite small, seating only 2,156 operagoers as opposed to 3,500 at La Scala in Milan and

3,700 at the New York Met. But backstage it is vast, with ample dressing rooms for hundreds of performers, workshops, canteens, wardrobe departments and storage areas for complete theatrical backdrops so that entire sets fifty feet high and weighing many tons can be lowered and stored without being dismantled, then raised again to be installed when needed.

The point about the Paris Opera is that it was always designed as more than just for the performance of opera. Hence the relative smallness of the auditorium, for much of the nonworking space is taken up with reception halls, salons, sweeping staircases and areas fit to offer a glittering venue to great state occasions. It still has over 2,500 doors, which take the resident firemen more than two hours to check before they go home. In Garnier's day it employed a permanent staff of 1,500 (about 1,000 today) and was illuminated by 900 gaslight globes fed by ten miles of copper pipe. It was converted to electricity in stages through the 1880s.

This was the intensely dramatic building that caught Gaston Leroux's vivid imagination when he visited in 1910 and first heard talk that once, years earlier, there had been a phantom living in the building; that things simply went missing, that unexplained accidents had occurred and that a shadowy figure had occasionally been seen flitting from dark corners and always heading downwards to the catacombs where none dared follow. From these twenty-year-old rumors Leroux created his story.

PREFACE

Old Gaston seems to have been the sort of man with whom one would love to take a drink at some Parisian café if only the ninety interceding years could be breached. He was big, jovial, bluff and cheerful: a bon viveur and generous host, wildly eccentric, with a pair of pince-nez glasses perched on his nose to compensate for poor eyesight.

He was born in 1868 and though from Normandy he actually arrived in the world during a train change in Paris when his mother was caught short. He was clever at school and in the manner of clever boys in middle-class France was destined to be a lawyer, being sent back to Paris to study law at the age of eighteen. It was a study he had no taste for at all. He was twenty-one when he graduated and the same year his father died, leaving him a million francs, which was a considerable fortune in those days. Hardly had Papa been popped belowground when young Gaston went on the town in quite a big way. Within six months he had got through the lot!

It was journalism, not the law courts, that beckoned, so he got a job as a reporter with *Echo de Paris* and later *Le Matin*. He found a love of theater and did some drama criticism but it was his knowledge of the law that made him a star court reporter and required him to witness a number of executions by guillotine. This made him a lifelong opponent of capital punishment, a most unusual outlook in those days. He showed ingenuity and audacity in obtaining scoop after scoop over the competition and obtained hard-to-get interviews with celebrities. *Le Matin* rewarded him with a commission as a wandering foreign correspondent.

These were the days when readers had no objection to a foreign correspondent having a pretty vivid imagination and it was not unknown for a journalist far from home, unable to get the facts of a story, simply to make it up. There is a glorious example of the American from Hearst Newspapers who arrived by train somewhere in the Balkans to cover a civil war. Unfortunately he overslept on the train and woke up in the next capital down the line, which happened to be pretty quiet. Rather perplexed, he recalled he had been sent to cover a civil war so he had better do it. He duly filed a vigorous war report. The next morning this was read by the embassy in Washington, who duly sent the report back to their masters at home. While the Hearst man slept on, the local government mobilized the militia. The peasants, fearing a pogrom, revolted. A civil war duly began. The journalist woke up to a telegram from New York congratulating him on a world scoop. It was into this ethos that Gaston Leroux fitted like a duck to water.

But travel then was harder and more tiring than now. After ten years covering stories across Europe, Russia, Asia and Africa he had become a celebrity but was exhausted. In 1907, aged thirty-nine, he decided to settle down and write novels. None in fact were more than what we would today call potboilers, which is probably why virtually nothing he wrote is easily available. Most of his stories were thrillers and for these he invented his own detective; but his creation never became Sherlock Holmes, his own personal icon. Still, he made a good living, enjoyed every moment of it, spent his advances as fast as the publishers could produce them, and churned out sixty-three books in his twenty years of professional writing. He died aged fifty-nine in 1927, just two years after Carl Laemmle's version of *The Phantom of the Opera* starring Lon Chaney received its premiere and went on to become a classic.

Looking at his original text today, frankly one is in a quandary. The basic idea is there and it is brilliant, but the way poor Gaston tells it is a mess. He begins with an introduction, above his own name, claiming that every line and word is true. Now, that is a very dangerous thing to do. To claim quite clearly that a work of fiction is absolutely true and therefore a historical record is to offer oneself as a hostage to fortune and to the skeptical reader, because from that moment on every single claim made that can be checked must be absolutely true. Leroux breaks this rule on almost every page.

An author *can* start a story cold, seemingly recounting true history but without saying so, leaving the reader guessing as to whether what he is reading truly happened or not. Thus is created that blend of truth and invention now called *faction*. A useful ploy in this methodology is to intersperse the fiction with genuinely true interludes that the reader can either recall or check out. Then the puzzlement in the reader's mind deepens but the author remains innocent of an outright lie. But there is a golden rule to this: everything you say must either be provably true or completely unprovable either way. For example, an author might write: "At dawn on the morning of September 1, 1939, fifty divisions of Hitler's army invaded Poland. At that same hour a soft-spoken man with perfectly forged papers arrived from Switzerland at Berlin's main station and disappeared into the waking city."

The first is a historical fact and the second cannot now be either proved or disproved. With a bit of luck the reader will believe both are true and read on. Leroux however begins by telling us that what he has in store is nothing but the truth and buttresses this with claims of conversations with witnesses of the actual events, perusal of records, and newly discovered (by him) diaries never seen before.

But his narration then hares off in all sorts of different directions, down blind alleys and back again, passing by a host of unexplained mysteries, unsupported claims and factual howlers until one is seized by the urge to do what Andrew Lloyd Webber did. This is, take a large blue pencil and trim out the rather breathless diversions to haul the story back to what is, after all, an amazing but credible tale.

Having been so critical of M. Leroux it would be only right and proper to justify one's censures with a few examples. Quite early in his narrative he refers to the Phantom as Erik but without ever explaining how he learned this. The Phantom was hardly in the habit of small talk and was not accustomed to go about introducing himself. As it happens, Leroux was right and we can only surmise he learned this name from Mme. Giry, of whom more anon.

Much more bewildering, Leroux tells his entire story without ever giving a date when it happened. For an investigative reporter, which he purports to be, this is a bizarre omission. The nearest clue is a single phrase in his own introduction. Here he says: "The events do not date more than thirty years back."

This has led some critics to subtract thirty years from the appearance in 1911 of his book and presume the year 1881. But "not more than" can also mean considerably less than, and there are several small clues that indicate the date of his story was probably much later than 1881 and more likely around 1893. Chief among these clues is the affair of the complete power failure of the lights in both auditorium and stage area, which lasted only a few seconds.

According to Leroux, the Phantom, outraged by his rejection by Christine, the girl he loved with an obsessive passion, chose to abduct her. For maximum effect the moment he selected was when she was on center stage in a performance of *Faust*. In the musical, Lloyd Webber has changed this to *Don Juan Triumphant*, an opera entirely composed by the Phantom himself. The lights suddenly failed, plunging the theater into pitch-darkness, and when they went up again, she was gone. Now, this cannot be done with nine hundred gas globes.

True, a mysterious saboteur who knew his way around could pull the master lever shutting off the gas supply to this host of globes. But they would extinguish in sequence as the gas supply ran out and after much spluttering and popping. Worse, as automatic reignition was not known then, they could only be relit by someone going round with a taper. That was what the humble profession of lamplighter was all about. The only way to produce utter darkness at the pull of a switch, and illumination again in another millisecond, is to operate the master control of a fully electric lighting system. This puts the date rather later than Leroux would have it.

He appears also to have made an error with the position, appearance and intelligence of Mme. Giry, an error corrected in the Lloyd Webber musical. His lady appears in the original book as a half-witted cleaner. She was in fact the mistress of the chorus and the corps de ballet, who hid behind the veneer of a starchy martinet (necessary to control a corps of excitable girls) a most courageous and compassionate nature.

One must forgive Leroux for this, for he was relying on human memory, that of his informants, and they were clearly describing another woman. But any policeman or court reporter will happily confirm that witnesses in court, honest and upright people, have some difficulty agreeing with each other and recalling with precision the events they witnessed last month, let alone eighteen years ago.

In a much more glaring error, M. Leroux describes a moment when the Phantom in another fit of pique causes the entire chandelier above the auditorium to crash down upon the audience, killing a single woman sitting beneath. That this lady turns out to be the woman hired to replace the Phantom's dismissed friend Mme. Giry is a lovely storyteller's touch. But he then goes on to say that this chandelier weighed 200,000 kilograms. That would be over 440,000 pounds, enough to bring it and half the ceiling down every night. The chandelier actually weighs seven tons; it did when it went up, it is still there, and it still does!

But far and away the most bizarre departure by Leroux from even the most basic rules of investigation and reporting is his end-of-book seduction by a mysterious character known only as "the Persian." This strange mountebank is briefly mentioned twice in the first two-thirds of the story, and in a most passing manner. Yet after the abduction of the soprano from center stage Leroux allows this man to take over the whole narrative and tell the entire story through his own eyes for the last third of the book. And what an implausible story it is.

Yet Leroux never attempts to cross-check his allegations. Although the young Vicomte Raoul de Chagny was supposed to have been present at every stage of the events described by the Persian, Leroux claims he could not find the Vicomte later to check the story. Of course he could have!

We will never know why the Persian had such a loathing of the Phantom but he produced a character assassination of the man that blackened him to the very gates of hell. Prior to the intervention of the Persian, Leroux the writer and most readers might have felt some human sympathy for the Phantom. Clearly he was monstrously disfigured in a society that too often equates ugliness with sin, but that was not his fault. He was evidently filled with hatred of society but, rejected and an exile, he must have had a truly appalling life. Until the Persian, we can see Erik as the Beast to the singer Christine's Beauty, but not intrinsically evil.

The Persian however paints him as a raging sadist; a serial killer and strangler for pleasure; one who delights in designing torture chambers and spying through a peephole on the wretches dying in agony within them; a man who worked for years in the service of the equally sadistic empress of Persia, devising for her ever more revolting torments to inflict on her prisoners.

According to the Persian he and the young aristocrat, descending to the lowest cellars to try to recover the kidnapped Christine, were themselves captured, imprisoned in a torture room, almost fried alive, but then miraculously escaped, fainted and woke up safe and sound. So also did Christine. It is a truly farcical story. Yet at the end of the book

Leroux admits he harbors a certain sympathy for the Phantom, a sentiment utterly impossible if one believes the Persian. But in every other detail Leroux seems to have swallowed the Persian's farrago of lies hook, line and sinker.

Fortunately there is one flaw in the Persian's story so glaring as to permit us to disbelieve the whole lot. He claimed that Erik had had a long and fulfilling life before coming to dwell in the cellars beneath the opera house. According to the Persian this grotesquely disfigured man had traveled widely through Western, Central and Eastern Europe, far into Russia, and down to the Persian Gulf. He then returned to Paris and became a contractor in the building of the Paris Opera under Garnier. This allegation has to be nonsense.

If the man had enjoyed such a life over so many years he would certainly have come to terms with his own disfigurement. To have been a contractor in the building of the opera house he would have had to conduct many business meetings, confront commissioning architects, negotiate with subcontractors and workers. Why on earth should he then decide to flee into exile underground because he could not face other members of the human race? Such a man, with his astuteness and intelligence, would have made a tidy packet from his contracting work and then retired in comfort to a walled residence in the countryside to live out his days in self-willed isolation, attended perhaps by a house servant immune to his ugliness.

PREFACE

The only logical step for a modern analyst to take, as Andrew Lloyd Webber has already done with the musical, is to discount the Persian's accounts and allegations in their totality, and never more so than in disbelieving both the Persian and Leroux that the Phantom died shortly after the events narrated. The sensible path to follow is to return to the basics and to those things we can actually know or presume on the basis of logic. And these are:

That sometime in the 1880s a desperately disfigured wretch, fleeing from contact with a society he felt loathed and reviled him, ran for sanctuary and took up residence in the labyrinth of cellars and storerooms beneath the Paris Opera. This is not so crazy a notion. Prisoners have survived many years in underground dungeons. But seven stories spread over three acres is not exactly close confinement. Even the underground sections of the Opera (and when the building was completely vacated he could wander through the upper levels undisturbed) are like a small city, with everything needed to establish a life-support system.

That over the years rumors began to grow and develop among impressionable and gullible staff that too many things went missing, and that a shadowy figure had occasionally been surprised before fleeing into the darkness. Again, not so crazy. Such rumors usually abound in rather spooky buildings.

That in the year 1893 something strange happened, which ended the Phantom's kingdom in the darkness. Peering from a closed box at the Opera on-stage, which he was wont to do, he spotted a lovely young understudy and fell hopelessly in love with her. Being self-taught after listening for years to the finest voices in Europe, he coached the young woman until one night, taking over the role from the leading diva, she set all Paris by its ears through the clarity and purity of her singing. Again, nothing impossible here, for overnight stardom through the revelation of a blazing but hitherto unsuspected talent is the stuff of which show-business legends are made, and there are many.

That the events moved to tragedy because the Phantom hoped that Christine might return his love. But she was courted by, and fell in love with, a handsome young viscount, Raoul de Chagny. Driven to extremes by rage and jealousy, the Phantom abducted his young soprano from the very stage of the Opera in mid-performance and took her to his sanctuary at the seventh and deepest level of the catacombs by the edge of that buried lake.

And there something passed between them, though we know not what. Then the young viscount, driven beyond fear of the dark and the caves, appeared to rescue her. Given a choice, Christine chose her Adonis. The Phantom had the chance to kill them both but, as the vengeful mob from above with a hundred burning torches to illuminate the darkness began to appear, he spared the lovers and disappeared into the last remaining shadows.

But before he did so she returned to him a single gold ring that he had earlier given her as a token of his love. And he left behind, for his persecutors to find, a mocking memento: a music box in the form of a monkey that played a tune called "Masquerade."

This is the story of the Lloyd Webber musical and it is the only one to make sense. The Phantom, broken and rejected once more, simply vanished and was never heard of again.

Or . . . was he?

ONE

THE CONFESSION OF ANTOINETTE GIRY

HOSPICE OF THE SISTERS OF CHARITY
OF THE ORDER OF ST.-VINCENT-DE-PAUL,
PARIS, SEPTEMBER 1906

There is a crack in the plaster of the ceiling far above my head and close to it a spider is creating a web. Strange to think this spider will outlive me, be here when I am gone, a few hours from now. Good luck, little spider, making a web to catch a fly to feed your babies.

How did it come to this? That I, Antoinette Giry, at the age of fifty-eight, am lying on my back in a hospice for the people of Paris, run by the good sisters, waiting to meet my Maker? I do not think I have been a very good person, not good like these sisters who clean up the endless mess, bound by their oath of poverty, chastity, humility and obedience. I could never have managed that. They have faith, you see. I was never able to have that faith. Is it time I learned it now? Probably. For I shall be gone before the night sky fills that small high window over there at the edge of my vision.

I am here, I suppose, because I simply ran out of money. Well, almost. There is a little bag under my pillow which no one knows about. But that is for a special purpose. Forty years ago I was a ballerina, so slim and young and beautiful then. So they told me, the young men who came to the stage door. And handsome they were too, those clean, sweet-smelling hard young bodies that could give and take so much pleasure.

And the most beautiful was Lucien. All the chorus called him Lucien le Bel, with a face to make a girl's heart hammer like a tambour. He took me out one sunny Sunday to the Bois de Boulogne and proposed, on one knee as it should be done, and I accepted him. One year later he was killed by the Prussian guns at Sedan. Then I wanted no more of marriage for a long time, nearly five years while I danced at the ballet.

I was twenty-eight when it ended, the dancing career. For one thing I had met Jules and we married and I became heavy with little Meg. More to the point, I was losing my litheness. Senior dancer of the corps fighting every day to stay slim and supple. But the Director was very good to me, a kind man. The Mistress of the Chorus was retiring; he said I had the experience and he did not wish to look outside the Opera for her

successor. He appointed me. *Maîtresse du corps de ballet.*
As soon as Meg was born and put with a wet nurse I
took up my duties. It was 1876, one year after the
opening of Garnier's new and magnificent opera house.
At last we were out of those cramped shoe boxes in
the rue le Peletier, the war was well over, the damage
to my beloved Paris repaired and life was good.

I did not even mind when Jules met his fat Belgian
and ran off to the Ardennes. Good riddance. At least
I had a job, which was more than he could ever say.
Enough to keep my small apartment, raise Meg and
nightly watch my girls delighting every crowned head
in Europe. I wonder what happened to Jules? Too late
to start enquiring now. And Meg? A ballet dancer and
chorus girl like her mama—I could at least do that for
her—until the awful fall ten years ago which left the
right knee stiff forever. Even then she was lucky, with
a bit of help from me. Dresser and personal maid to
the greatest diva in Europe, Christine de Chagny.
Well, if you discount that uncouth Australian Melba,
which I do. I wonder where Meg is now? Milan, Rome,
Madrid perhaps. Where the diva is singing. And to
think I once used to shout at the Vicomtesse de
Chagny to pay attention and stay in line!

So what am I doing here, waiting for a too-early
grave? Well, there was retirement eight years ago, on
my fiftieth birthday. They were very nice about it. The
usual platitudes. And a generous bonus for my twenty-
two years as mistress. Enough to live on. Plus a little
private coaching for the incredibly clumsy daughters of

the rich. Not much but enough, and a little put by. Until last spring.

That was when the pains began, not many at first but sharp and sudden, deep in the lower stomach. They gave me bismuth for indigestion and charged a small fortune. I did not know then that the steel crab was in me, driving his great claws into me and always growing as he fed. Not until July. Then it was too late. So I lie here, trying not to scream with the pain, waiting for the next spoonful of the white goddess, the powder that comes from the poppies of the East.

Not long to wait now for the final sleep. I am not even afraid anymore. Perhaps He will be merciful? I hope so, but surely He will take away the pain. I try to concentrate on something else. I look back and think of all the girls I trained, and my pretty young Meg with her stiff knee waiting to find her man—I hope she finds a good one. And of course I think of my boys, my two lovely tragic boys. I think of them most of all.

"Madame, Monsieur l'Abbé is here."

"Thank you, Sister. I cannot see too well. Where is he?"

"I am here, my child, Father Sebastien. By your side. Do you feel my hand on your arm?"

"Yes, Father."

"You should make your peace with God, *ma fille*. I am ready to take your confession."

"It is time. Forgive me, Father, for I have sinned."

"Tell me, my child. Keep nothing back."

"There was a time, long ago, in the year 1882, when I did something that changed many lives. I did not know then what would happen. I acted on impulse and for motives I thought to be good. I was thirty-four, the mistress of the corps de ballet at the Paris Opera. I was married but my husband had deserted me and run off with another woman."

"You must forgive them, my child. Forgiveness is a part of penitence."

"Oh, I do, Father. Long since. But I had a daughter, Meg, then six years old. There was a fair out at Neuilly and I took her one Sunday. There were calliopes and carousels, steam engines and performing monkeys who collected centimes for the hurdy-gurdy man. Meg had never seen a circus before. But there was also a show of freaks. A line of tents with notices advertising the world's strongest man, the acrobat dwarves, a man so covered in tattoos that one could not see his skin, a black man with a bone through his nose and pointed teeth, a lady with a beard.

"At the end of the line was a sort of cage on wheels, with bars spaced almost a foot apart, and filthy reeking straw on the floor. It was bright in the sun but dark in the cage so I peered in to see what animal it contained. I heard the clank of chains and saw something lying huddled in the straw. Just then a man came up.

"He was big and beefy, with a red, crude face. He carried a tray on a sash round his neck. It contained lumps of horse manure collected from where the ponies were tethered, and pieces of rotten fruit. 'Have a go, lady,' he said, 'see if you can pelt the monster. One centime a throw.' Then he turned to the cage and shouted, 'Come on, come near the front or you know what you'll get.' The chains clanked again, and something more animal than human shuffled into the light, nearer to the bars.

"I could see that it was indeed human, though hardly so. A male in rags, crusted with filth, gnawing on an old piece of apple. Apparently he had to live on what people threw over him. Ordure and feces clung to his thin body. There were manacles on his wrists and ankles and the steel had bitten into the flesh to leave open wounds where maggots writhed. But it was the face and head that caused Meg to burst into tears.

"The skull and face were hideously deformed, the former displaying only a few tufts of filthy hair. The face was distorted down one side as if struck long ago by a monstrous hammer and the flesh of this visage was raw and shapeless like molten candle wax. The eyes were deep set in sockets puckered and misshapen. Only half of the mouth and a section of jaw on one side had escaped the deformation and looked like a normal human face.

"Meg was holding a toffee apple. I do not know why, but I took it from her, walked to the bars and held it out. The beefy man went into a rage, screaming and shouting that I was depriving him of his living. I ignored him and pushed the toffee apple into the filthy hands behind the bars. And I looked into the eyes of this deformed monster.

"Father, thirty-five years ago when the ballet was suspended during the Franco-Prussian War, I was among those who tended the young wounded coming back from the front. I have seen men in agony, I have heard them scream. But I have never seen pain like I saw in those eyes."

"Pain is part of the human condition, my child. But what you did that day with the toffee apple was not a sin but an act of compassion. I must hear your sins if I am to give absolution."

"But I went back that night and I stole him."

"You did what?"

"I went to the old shuttered opera house, took a heavy pair of bolt cutters from the carpentry shop and a large cowled cloak from wardrobe, hired a hansom cab and returned to Neuilly. The fairgrounds was deserted in the moonlight, the performers asleep in their caravans. There were curs who started to bark, but I threw them scraps of meat. I found the cage trailer, withdrew the iron bar that held it closed, opened the door and called softly inside.

"The creature was chained to one wall. I cut the chains on wrists and feet and urged him to come out. He seemed terrified, but when he saw me in the moonlight, he shuffled out and dropped to the ground. I covered him in the cloak, pulled the cowl over that dreadful head and led him away to the coach. The driver grumbled at the awful smell, but I paid him extra and he drove us back to my flat behind the rue le Peletier. Was taking him away a sin?"

"Certainly it was an offense in law, my child. He belonged to the fair owner, brutal though the man may have been. As to an offense before God . . . I do not know. I think not."

"There is more, Father. Have you the time?"

"You are facing eternity. I think I can spare a few minutes, but recall there may be others dying here who will also need me."

"I hid him in my small flat for a month, Father. He took a bath, the first in his life, then another and many more. I disinfected the open wounds and bandaged them so that they slowly healed. I gave him clothes from my husband's chest and food so that he recovered his health. He also for the first time in his life slept in a real bed with sheets—I moved Meg in with me, which was a good thing to do because she was terrified of him. I found that he was himself petrified with fear if anyone came to the door and would scuttle away to hide under the stairs. I also found that he could talk, in French but with an Alsatian accent, and slowly over that month he told me his story.

"He was born Erik Muhlheim, just forty years ago. In Alsace which was then French but soon to be an-nexed by Germany. He was the only son of a circus family, living in a caravan, constantly moving from town to town.

"He told me that he had learned in early childhood the circumstances of his birth. The midwife had screamed when she saw the tiny child emerging into the world, for he was even then horribly disfigured. She handed the squealing bundle to the mother and ran away, yelling (foolish cow) that she had delivered the devil himself.

"So poor Erik arrived, destined from birth to be hated and rejected by people who believe that ugliness is the outward show of sinfulness.

"His father was the circus carpenter, engineer and handyman. It was watching him at work that Erik first developed his talent for anything that could be constructed with tools and hands. It was in the sideshows that he saw the techniques of illusion, with mirrors, trapdoors and secret passages that would later play such a part in his life in Paris.

"But his father was a drunken brute who whipped the boy constantly for the most minor offenses or none at all; his mother a useless besom who just sat in the corner and wailed. Spending most of his young life in pain and in tears, he tried to avoid the caravan and slept in the straw with the circus animals and especially the horses. He was seven, sleeping in the stables, when the big top caught fire.

"The fire ruined the circus, which went bankrupt. The staff and the artistes scattered to join other enterprises. Erik's father, without a job, drank himself to death. His mother ran away to become a servant in nearby Strasbourg. Running out of money for booze, his father sold him to the master of a passing freak show. He spent nine years in the wheeled cage, daily pelted with filth and ordure for the amusement of cruel crowds. He was sixteen when I found him."

"A pitiable tale, my child, but what has this to do with your mortal sins?"

"Patience, Father. Hear me out, you will understand, for no creature on the planet has ever heard the truth before. I kept Erik in my apartment for a month but it could not go on. There were neighbors, callers at the door. One night I took him to my place of work, the Opera, and he had found his new home.

"Here he had sanctuary at last, a place to hide where the world would never find him. Despite his terror of naked flame, he took a torch and went down into the lowest cellars where the darkness would hide his terrible face. With timber and tools from the carpenters' shop he built his home by the lake's edge. He furnished it with pieces from the props department, fabric from the wardrobe mistress. In the wee small hours when all was abandoned he could raid the staff canteen for food and even pilfer the directors' pantry for delicacies. And he read.

"He made a key to the Opera library and spent years giving himself that education he had never had; night after night by candlelight he devoured the library, which is enormous. Of course most of the works were of music and opera. He came to know every single opera ever written and every note of every aria. With his manual skills he created a maze of secret passages known only to himself and having practiced long ago with the tightrope walkers he could run along the highest and narrowest gantries without fear. For eleven years he lived there, and became a man underground.

"But of course before long rumors started and grew. Food, clothing, candles, tools went missing in the night. A credulous staff began to talk of a phantom in the cellars until finally every tiny accident—and back-stage many tasks are dangerous—came to be blamed on the mysterious phantom. Thus the legend started and grew."

"*Mon Dieu*, but I have heard of this. Ten years . . . no, it must be more . . . I was summoned to give the last rites to some poor wretch who was found hanged. Some-one told me then that the Phantom had done it."

"The man's name was Buquet, Father. But it was not Erik. Joseph Buquet was given to periods of great depression and certainly took his own life. At first I welcomed the rumors for I thought they would keep my poor boy—for thus I thought of him—safe in his small kingdom in the darkness below the Opera and perhaps they would have done, until that dreadful au-tumn of '93. He did something very foolish, Father. He fell in love.

"Then she was called Christine Daae. You probably know her today as Madame la Vicomtesse de Chagny."

"But this is impossible. Not . . ."

"Yes, the same one, then a chorus girl in my charge. Not much of a dancer, but a clear, pure voice. But untrained. Erik had listened night after night to the greatest voices in the world; he had studied the texts, he knew how she should be coached. When he had finished, she took over the leading role one night and by morning had become a star.

"My poor, ugly, outcast Erik thought she might love him in return but of course it was impossible. For she had her own young love. Driven by despair Erik abducted her one night, from the very center of the stage, in the middle of his own opera, *Don Juan Triumphant.*"

"But all Paris heard of this scandal, even a humble priest like me. A man was killed."

"Yes, Father. The tenor Piangi. Erik did not mean to kill him, just to keep him quiet. But the Italian choked and died. Of course it was the end. By chance the Commissioner of Police was in the audience that night. He summoned a hundred gendarmes; they took blazing torches and with a mob of vengeance-seekers descended into the cellars, right to the level of the lake itself.

"They found the secret stairs, the passages, the house by the lake, and they found Christine shocked and swooning. She was with her suitor the young Vicomte de Chagny, dear, sweet Raoul. He took her away and comforted her as only a man can, with strong arms and gentle caresses.

"Two months later she was found with child. So he married her, gave her his name, his title, his love and the necessary wedding band. The son was born in the summer of '94 and they have brought him up together. And she went on these past twelve years to become the greatest diva in all Europe."

"But they never found Erik, my child? No trace of the Phantom, I seem to recall."

"No, Father, they never found him. But I did. I returned desolate to my small office behind the chorus room. When I drew aside the curtain of my wardrobe niche, there he was, the mask he always wore, even alone, clutched in his hand, crouching in the dark as he used to beneath the stairs at my apartment eleven years before."

"And of course you told the police. . . ."

"No, Father, I did not. He was still my boy, one of my two boys. I could not hand him over to the mob again. So I took a woman's hat and heavy veil, a long cloak. . . . We walked side by side down the staff staircase and turn out into the street, just two women fleeing into the night. There were hundreds of others. No one took any notice.

"I kept him for three months at my apartment half a mile away, but the 'wanted' notices were everywhere. And a price on his head. He had to leave Paris, leave France entirely."

"You helped him to escape, my child. That was a crime and a sin."

"Then I will pay for it, Father. Soon now. That winter was bitter cold and hard. To take a train was out of the question. I hired a diligence, four horses and a closed carriage. To Le Havre. There I left him hidden in cheap lodgings while I scoured the docks and their seedy bars. Finally I found a sea captain, master of a small freighter bound for New York and one to take a bribe and ask no questions. So one night in mid-January 1894, I stood on the end of the longest quay and watched the stern lights of the tramp steamer disappear into the darkness, bound for the New World. Tell me, Father, is there someone else with us? I cannot see but I feel someone here."

"Indeed, there is a man who has just entered."

"I am Armand Dufour, madame. A novice came to my chambers and said that I was needed here."

"And you are a notary and commissioner for oaths?"

"Indeed I am, madame."

"Monsieur Dufour, I wish you to reach beneath my pillow. I would do so myself but I am become too weak. Thank you. What do you find?"

"Why, a letter of some sort, enclosed in a fine manila envelope. And a small bag of chamois leather."

"Precisely. I wish you to take pen and ink and sign across the sealed flap that this letter has been delivered into your charge this day, and has not been opened by you or anyone else."

"My child, I beg you hurry. We have not finished our business."

"Patience, Father. I know my time is short but after so many years of silence I must now struggle to complete the course. Are you done, Monsieur le Notaire?"

"It has been written just as you requested, madame."

"And on the front of the envelope?"

"I see, written in what must surely be your own hand, the words: M. Erik Muhlheim, New York City."

"And the small leather bag?"

"I have it in my hand."

"Open it if you please."

"*Nom d'un chien!* Gold Napoleons. I have not seen these since . . ."

"But they are still valid tender?"

"Certainly, and most valuable."

"Then I wish you to take them all, and the letter, and take it to New York City and deliver it. Personally."

"Personally? In New York? But madame, I do not usually . . . I have never been . . ."

"Please, Monsieur le Notaire. There is enough gold? For five weeks away from the office?"

"More than enough, but—"

"My child, you cannot know this man is still alive."

"Oh, he will have survived, Father. He will always survive."

"But I have no address for him. Where to find him?"

"Ask, Monsieur Dufour. Search the immigration records. The name is rare enough. He will be there somewhere. A man who wears a mask to hide his face."

"Very well, madame. I will try. I will go there and I will try. But I cannot guarantee success."

"Thank you. Tell me, Father, has one of the sisters administered to me a spoonful of tincture of a white powder?"

"Not in the hour that I have been here, *ma fille*. Why?"

"It is strange but the pain has gone. Such beautiful,

sweet relief. I cannot see to either side but I can see a sort of tunnel and an arch. My body was in such pain but now it hurts no more. It was so cold but now there is warmth everywhere."

"Do not delay, Monsieur l'Abbé. She is leaving us."

"Thank you, Sister. I hope I may know my duty."

"I am walking towards the arch, there is light at the end. Such sweet light. Oh, Lucien, are you there? I am coming, my love."

"In Nomine Patris, et Filii, et Spiritus Sancti . . ."

"Hurry, Father."

"Ego te absolvo ab omnibus peccatis tuis."

"Thank you, Father."

TWO

THE CHANT OF ERIK MULHEIM

PENTHOUSE SUITE, E. M. TOWER, PARK ROW,
MANHATTAN, OCTOBER 1906

Every day, summer or winter, rain or shine, I rise early. I dress and come up from my quarters to this small square rooftop terrace atop the pinnacle of the highest skyscraper in all New York. From here, depending upon which side of the square I stand, I can look west across the Hudson River towards the open green lands of New Jersey. Or north towards the midtown and up-town sections of this amazing island so full of wealth and filth, extravagance and poverty, vice and crime. Or south towards the open sea, which leads back to Europe and the bitter road I have traveled. Or east across the river to Brooklyn and, lost in the sea mist, the lunatic enclave called Coney Island, the original source of my wealth.

And, I, who spent seven years terrorized by a brutish father, nine an animal chained in a cage, eleven an outcast in the cellars below the Paris Opera and ten fighting my way up from the fish-gutting sheds of Gravesend Bay to this eminence, know that I now have wealth and power beyond the dreams of Croesus. So I look down on this sprawling city and I think: how I hate and despise you, Human Race.

It was a long hard voyage that brought me here in the first days of 1894. The Atlantic was wild with storms. I lay in my cot sick unto death, my passage prepaid by that one kind person I have ever met, tolerating the sneers and insults of the crew, knowing they could tip me overboard in a trice, and none the wiser, if I attempted to respond, borne up only by the rage and hatred for them all. Four weeks we rolled and thumped our way across the ocean until one bitter night at the end of January the sea calmed and we were dropping anchor in the Roads ten miles south of the tip of Manhattan Island.

Of this I knew nothing, save that we had arrived. Somewhere. But I heard the crew in their harsh Breton accent telling each other that in the dawn we would move up into the East River and dock for customs inspection. Then I knew I would be discovered again; exposed, humiliated, rejected as an immigrant and sent back in chains.

In the small hours, when everyone was asleep including the drunken night watch, I took a moldy life belt from the deck and went over the edge into the icy sea. I had seen lights dimly flickering in the blackness, how far I did not know. But I began to drive my frozen body towards them and an hour later pulled myself up onto a sandy beach crusted with frost. I did not know it, but my first steps in the New World were on the beach at Gravesend Bay, Coney Island.

The lights I had seen came from guttering oil lamps in the windows of some miserable shacks at the top of the beach, beyond the tide line, and when I stumbled towards them and looked through the filthy panes I saw rows of huddled men skinning and gutting fresh-caught fish. Further down the line of huts there was an empty space in the middle of which burned a great bonfire and round it a dozen wretches were crouched, drawing the heat into their bodies. Half-dead from cold, I knew I too must share that heat or freeze to death. I walked into the light of the great fire, felt the wave of heat and looked at them. My mask was stuffed inside my clothes, this terrible head and face was lit by the flames. They turned and stared at me.

I have hardly ever laughed in my life. There has been no cause to. But that night in the subzero predawn cold I laughed inside myself for sheer relief. They looked at me . . . and took no notice. For one way or another every one of them was deformed. By a sheer chance I had come upon the nightly encampment of the Outcasts of Gravesend Bay, the rejects who could only make a miserable living by gutting and cleaning fish while the fishermen and the city slept.

So they let me dry and warm myself by their fire and asked me where I had come from, though it was obvious I had come from the sea. From reading the texts of all the English operas I had learned a few words of this language and told them I had fled from France. It made no difference, they had all fled from somewhere, pursued by society to this last desolate sand spit. They called me Frenchie and let me join them, sleeping in the shacks on piles of stinking nets, working through the nights for a few dimes, living on scraps, often cold and hungry, but safe from the law and its chains and jails.

Spring came and I began to learn what lay beyond the tangle of bayberry and scrub oak that screened the fishing village from the rest of Coney Island. I learned the whole island was lawless, or rather a law unto itself. Not incorporated into the City of Brooklyn across the narrow strait, and until recently ruled by a half-politician, half-gangster called John McKane, who had just been arrested. But McKane's legacy lived on in this lunatic island dedicated to funfairs, brothels, crime, vice and pleasure. The last was the aim of the bourgeois New Yorkers who came each weekend and before they had left spent fortunes on foolish diversions laid on for them by the entrepreneurs who had the wit to provide those pleasures.

Unlike the rest of the Outcasts who would gut fish

for all of their lives and never rise above it through their own doltish stupidity, I knew that with wit and ingenuity I could get out of these shacks and make a fortune from the pleasure parks even then being planned and built further along the island. But how? First, in darkness, I crept into the town and stole clothes, proper clothes, from washing lines and empty beach cottages. Then I took lumber from the building sites and built a better shack. But with my face I could still not move by daylight into that raucous unruled society where tourists were happily fleeced of fortunes each weekend.

A new arrival came to join us, hardly more than a boy of seventeen, ten years my junior but old beyond his years. Unlike most he was physically unscarred, undeformed, with a bone-pale face and black expressionless eyes. He came from Malta and had an education, learned from the Catholic fathers there. He spoke fluent English, knew Latin and Greek and had not a shred of scruple in him. He was here because, driven to rage by the endless penances inflicted on him by priests, he had taken a kitchen knife and plunged it into his tutor, killing him instantly. On the run, he had fled Malta to the Barbary Coast, served a while as a pleasure-boy in a house of sodomy, then stowed away on a ship that by chance was headed for New York. But he still had a price on his head so he avoided the immigration filter at Ellis Island and drifted downwards to Gravesend Bay.

I needed a front man who could do my bidding in

daylight; he needed my ingenuity and skills to get us out of this place. He became my subordinate and representative in all things and together we have moved from those fish-gutting sheds to wealth and power over half New York and much beyond. To this day I know him only as Darius.

But if I taught him, he also taught me, converting me from old and foolish beliefs to worship of the one and only true god, the Great Master who has never let me down.

The problem of my being able to move in daylight was solved most simply. In the summer of '94, with savings scrimped from the fish-cleaning job, I had a craftsman make up a latex mask to fit over my whole head with just holes for eyes and mouth. The mask of a clown, with bulbous red nose and wide gap-toothed smile. With baggy jacket and pantaloons I could move through the midway unsuspected. People with children even waved and smiled. The clown outfit was my passport into the daylight world. For two years we just made money. There were so many scams and frauds that I forget how many I invented.

The simplest were often the best. I discovered that each weekend the tourists despatched 250,000 postcards from Coney Island. Most sought a place to buy stamps. So I bought postcards for one cent, stamped the words Postage Paid on them and sold them for two. The tourists were happy. They did not know that postage was free anyway. But I wanted more, much more.

I could sense a boom in mass entertainment coming that would prove a licence to print one's own money.

In that first year and a half I suffered only one reverse, but it was a bad one. Returning home to the shacks one night with a bag full of dollars, I was set upon by a crowd of four footpads armed with cudgels and brass knuckles. Had they just robbed me of my money it would have been bad but not life threatening. But they tore off my clown's mask, saw my face and beat me until I almost died.

It took me a month in my cot till I could walk again. Since then I have carried a small derringer on my person at all times, for as I lay there I swore that no one would ever hurt me again and get away with it.

By the winter I had heard of a man called Paul Boyton. He was seeking to open the island's first enclosed all-weather amusement park. I instructed Darius to arrange to meet him and to present himself as a designing engineer of genius fresh arrived from Europe. It worked. Boyton commissioned a series of six amusement rides for his new enterprise. I designed them of course, using deception, optical illusion and engineering skill to create sensations of fear and bewilderment among the tourists, all of which they loved. Boyton opened Sea Lion Park in 1895 and the crowds flocked in.

Boyton wanted to pay Darius for "his" inventions, but I stopped him. Instead I demanded ten cents on the dollar for everything earned by those six rides, for a period of ten years. Boyton had sunk everything he had into his funfair and was deep in debt. Within a month those rides, monitored by Darius, were bringing in a hundred dollars a week to us alone. But there was much more to come.

The successor to political boss McKane was a red-haired firebrand called George Tilyou. He too wanted to open an amusement park and cash in on the boom. Regardless of the rage of Boyton, who could do nothing about it, I designed even more ingenious diversions for Tilyou's enterprise on the same basis, a percentage franchise. Steeplechase Park opened in 1897 and began to bring us a thousand dollars a day. By then I had bought and moved to a pleasant bungalow nearer to Manhattan Beach. Neighbors were few and mostly at weekends, times when I was, in my clown's costume, circulating freely among the tourists between the two amusement parks.

There were frequent boxing tournaments on Coney Island with very heavy betting by the millionaire gentry arriving on the new elevated train from Brooklyn Bridge to Manhattan Beach Hotel. I watched but did not gamble, convinced that most fights were fixed. Gambling was illegal throughout New York and Brooklyn, indeed all of New York State. But on Coney Island, last outpost of the crime frontier, huge sums changed hands as bookmakers took the gamblers' money. In 1899 Jim Jeffries challenged Bob Fitzsimmons for the world heavyweight title—on Coney Island. Our joint fortune was by then $250,000 and I intended to place it all on the challenger, Jeffries, at long odds. Darius almost went mad with rage until I explained my idea.

I had noticed that between rounds the fighters almost always took a long swig of fresh water from a bottle, sometimes but not always spitting it out. At my instruction Darius, masquerading as a sports reporter, simply switched Fitzsimmons's bottle for one laced with sedative. Jeffries knocked him out. I collected a million dollars. Later that year Jeffries defended his title against Sailor Tom Sharkey at the Coney Island Athletic Club. Same scam, same result. Poor Sharkey. We netted 2 million. It was time to move up-island and upmarket, for I had been studying the affairs of an even wilder and more lawless carnival for the making of money: the New York Stock Exchange. But there was still one last strike to be made on Coney Island.

Two hustlers called Frederic Thompson and Skip Dundy were desperate to open a third and even bigger amusement park. The first was an alcoholic engineer and the second a stuttering financier and so urgent was their need for cash that they were already into the banks for more than they were worth. I had Darius create a "shell" company, a loan corporation, which stunned them by offering an unsecured loan at zero interest. Instead, the E. M. Corporation wanted 10 percent of the gross take of Luna Park for a decade. They agreed. They had no choice; it was that or bankruptcy with a half-finished park. Luna Park opened on May 2, 1903. At 9:00 A.M. Thompson and Dundy were bankrupt. At sundown they had paid off all their debts—bar mine. Within the first four months Luna Park had grossed 5 million dollars. It leveled at a million a month and still does. By then we had moved to Manhattan.

I started in a modest brownstone house, staying inside most of the time for here the clown's disguise was useless. Darius joined the stock exchange on my behalf, following my instructions as I pored over corporate reports and the details of new share issues. It soon became plain that in this amazing country everything was booming. New ideas and projects, if skillfully promoted, were immediately subscribed. The economy was expanding at a lunatic rate, pushing westwards and ever westwards. With every new industry there was a demand for raw materials, along with ships and railroads to deliver them and haul away the product to the waiting markets.

Through the years I had been on Coney Island the immigrants had been pouring in by the million from every land to east and west. The Lower East Side, almost beneath my terrace as I now look down, was and remains a vast teeming cauldron of every race and creed living cheek by jowl in poverty, violence, vice and crime. Only a mile or two away the super-rich have their mansions, their coaches and their beloved opera.

By 1903 after a few mishaps I had mastered the intricacies of the stock market and worked out how the giants like Pierpont Morgan had made their fortunes. Like them I moved into coal in West Virginia, steel in Pittsburgh, railroads out to Texas, shipping from Savannah via Baltimore to Boston, silver in New Mexico and property throughout Manhattan Island. But I became better and harder than them, through single-minded worship of the only true god, to whom Darius had led me. For this is Mammon the god of gold who permits no mercy, no charity, no compassion and no scruple. There is no widow, no child, no pauper wretch who cannot be crushed a little more for a few extra granules of the precious metal that so pleases the Master. With the gold comes the power and with the power even more gold in one glorious world-conquering cycle.

In all things I am and remain Darius's master and superior. In all things save one. Never was created on this planet a colder or more cruel man. A creature more dead of soul never walked. In this he is beyond me. And yet he has his weakness. Just one. On a certain night, curious about his rare absences, I had him followed. He went to a den in the Moorish community and there took hashish until he was in a sort of trance. It seems this is his only flaw. Once I thought he might be my friend, but I long since learned he has but one; his worship of gold consumes him night and day, and he stays with me and loyal to me only because I can spin it in endless quantities.

By 1903 I had enough to undertake the construction of the highest skyscraper in New York, the E. M. Tower, on a vacant lot on Park Row. It was completed in 1904, forty stories of steel, concrete, granite and

glass. And the real beauty is that the thirty-seven stories let out beneath me have paid for it all and the
value has doubled. That leaves one suite for the corporation staff, linked by phone and ticker tape to the
markets; a floor above being half of it the apartment
of Darius and half the corporate boardroom; and above
them all my own penthouse with its upper terrace dom-
inating everything I can see and yet ensuring that I
myself cannot be seen.

So . . . my cage on wheels, my gloomy cellars have
become an eyrie in the sky where I can walk unmasked
and none to see my face from hell but the passing gulls
and the wind from the south. And from here I can
even see the finally finished and gleaming roof of my
one single indulgence, my one project that is not dedicated to making more money but to the extraction of
revenge.

Far in the distance at West Thirty-fourth Street
stands the newly completed Manhattan Opera House,
the rival that will set the snobby Metropolitan by the
ears. When I came here I wanted to see opera again,
but of course I needed a screened and curtained box
at the Met. The committee there, dominated by Mrs.
Astor and her cronies of the social register, the dam-
nable Four Hundred, required me to appear in person
for an interview. Impossible, of course. I sent Darius,
but they refused to accept him, demanding to see me
in person and face to face. They will pay for that insult.
For I found another opera-lover who had been
snubbed. Oscar Hammerstein, having already opened

one opera house and failed, was financing and designing a new one. I became his invisible partner. It will open in December and will wipe the floor with the Met. No expense will be spared. The great Gonci will star but most of all Melba herself, yes, Melba, will come and sing. Even now Hammerstein is at Garnier's Grand Hotel on the Boulevard des Capucines in Paris, spending my money to bring her to New York.

An unprecedented feat. I will make those snobs, the Vanderbilts, Rockefellers, Whitneys, Goulds, Astors and Morgans crawl before they listen to the great Melba.

For the rest, I look out and I look down. Yes, and back. A life of pain and rejection, of fear and hatred: you of me and I of you. Only one showed me kindness, took me from a cage to a cellar and then to a ship when the rest were hunting me like a winded fox; one who was like the mother I hardly had or knew.

And one other, whom I loved but who could not love me. You despise me for that also, Human Race? Because I could not make a woman love me as a man? But there was one moment, one short time, like Chesterton's donkey "one far fierce hour and sweet" when I thought I might be loved. . . . Ashes, cinders, nothing. Not to be. Never to be. So there can only be the other love, the devotion to the Master who never lets me down. And him I will worship all my life.

THREE

THE DESPAIR OF ARMAND DUFOUR

I hate this city. I should never have come. Why on earth did I come? Because of the wish of a woman dying in Paris who, for all I know, may well have been deranged. And for the bag of gold Napoleons, of course. But even that, perhaps I should never have taken it.

Where is this man to whom I am supposed to deliver a letter that makes no sense? All Father Sebastien could tell me was that he is hideously disfigured and should therefore be noticeable. But it is the reverse; he is invisible.

I am becoming every day more sure that he never got here. No doubt he was refused entry by the officers

at Ellis Island. I went there—what chaos. The whole
world of the poor and the dispossessed seems to be
pouring into this country and most of them remain
right here in this awful city. I have never seen so many
down-and-outs: columns of shabby refugees, smelly,
even louse-ridden from the voyage in stinking holds,
clutching ragged parcels with all their worldly posses-
sions, filing in endless ranks through those bleak buildings on that hopeless island. Towering over them all
from the other island is the statue that we gave them.
The lady with the torch. We should have told Bar-
tholdi to keep his damn statue in France and given the
Yankees something else instead. A good set of Larousse
dictionaries perhaps, so they could have learned a civilized language.

But no, we had to give them something symbolic.
Now they have turned it into a magnet for every der-
elict in Europe and far beyond to come flocking in here
looking for a better life. *Quelle blague!* They are crazy,
these Yankees. How do they ever expect to create a
nation by letting such people in? The rejects from
every country between Bantry Bay and Brest Litovsk,
from Trondheim to Taormina. What do they expect?
To make a rich and powerful nation one day out of
this rabble?

I went to see the Chief Immigration Officer. Thank
God, he had a French-speaker available. But he said
though few were turned back those clearly diseased or
deformed were rejected, so my man would almost certainly have been among that group. Even if he did get

in, it has been twelve years. He could be anywhere in this country and it is three thousand miles from east to west.

So I returned to the city authorities, but they pointed out there were five boroughs and virtually no residence records. The man could be in Brooklyn, Queens, Bronx, Staten Island. So I have no choice but to stay here on Manhattan Island and seek this runaway from justice. What a task for a good Frenchman!

They have records at city hall listing a dozen Muhlheims, and I have tried them all. If his name were Smith I would go home now. They even have many telephones here, and a list of those who own them, but no Erik Muhlheim. I have asked the taxation authorities but they say their records are confidential.

The police were better. I found an Irish sergeant who said he would search, for a fee. I know damn well the "fee" went into his trouser pocket. But he went away and came back to say that no Muhlheim had ever been in trouble with the police but he had half a dozen Mullers if that was any help. Imbecile.

There is a circus out on Long Island and I went there. Another blank. I tried their great hospital called Bellevue but they have no record of a man so deformed ever presenting himself for treatment. I can think of nowhere else to go.

I lodge in a modest hotel in the back streets behind this great boulevard. I eat their horrible stews and drink their awful beer. I sleep in a narrow cot and wish I was back in my apartment on the Île St. Louis, warm and comfortable and pressed against the fine fat but-tocks of Madame Dufour. It is getting colder and the money is running short. I want to return to my beloved Paris, to a civilized city where people walk instead of running everywhere, a place where the carriages drive sedately instead of racing like maniacs and the trams are not a danger to life and limb.

To make matters worse I thought I could speak some words of the perfidious language of Shakespeare, for I have seen and heard the English milords who come to race their horses at Auteuil and Chantilly, but here they speak through their noses and very, very fast.

Yesterday I saw an Italian coffee shop on this same street serving good mocha and even Chianti wine. Not Bordeaux, of course, but better than that piss-making Yankee beer. Ah, I see it even now, across this deadly dangerous street. I will take a good strong coffee for my nerves' sake, then return and book my passage home.

FOUR

THE
LUCK OF
CHOLLY BLOOM

I tell you guys, there are times when being a reporter in the fastest, hummingest city in the world is the greatest job on earth. Okay, we all know that there are hours and days of footslogging and nothing to show for it; leads that go nowhere, interviews rebuffed, no story. Right? Barney, can we have another round of beers here?

Yep, there are times when there's no scandal at city hall (not many, of course), no celebrity divorce, no bodies at dawn in Central Park, and life loses its sparkle. Then you think: what am I doing here, why am I wasting my time? Maybe I really should have taken over my dad's outfitters in Poughkeepsie. We all know the feeling.

But that's the point. That's what makes it better than selling men's pants in Poughkeepsie. Suddenly out of left field something happens and, if you're smart, you see a great story right within your grasp. Happened to me yesterday. Gotta tell you about it. Thanks, Barney.

It was in this coffee shop. You know Fellini's? On Broadway at Twenty-sixth. A bad day. Spent most of it chasing up a new lead on the Central Park murders and nothing. The mayor's office is screaming at the bureau of detectives and they have nothing new, so they're in a temper and saying nothing worth printing. I face the prospect of going back to the city desk to say I don't even have a column inch worth printing. So I thought I'll go in and have one of Papa Fellini's fudge sundaes. Plenty of syrup. You know the one? Keeps you going.

So it's crowded. I take the last booth. Ten minutes later a guy walks in looking miserable as sin. He looks around, sees I have a booth to myself and walks over. Very polite. Bows. I nod. He says something in a foreign lingo. I point to the spare chair. He sits down and orders a coffee. Only he doesn't pronounce it *kauphy*, he says *kaffay*. The waiter's Italian, so that's fine by him. Only I reckon this guy is probably French. Why? He just looked French. So, being polite, I greet him. In French.

Do I speak French? Is the Chief Rabbi Jewish? Well, all right, a little French. So I says to him, "Bon-jewer Mon-sewer." Just trying to be a good New Yorker.

Well, this Frenchie goes crazy. He launches into a torrent of French that is way above my head. And he's distressed, nearly in tears. Reaches into his pocket and brings out a letter, very important looking, with wax over the flap and a kind of seal. Waves it in my face.

Now at this point I am still trying to be nice to a visitor in distress. The temptation is to finish the ice cream, throw down a dime and get out of there. But instead I think, what the hell, let's try and help this guy because he seems to have a worse day than I have, and that is saying something. So I call over Papa Fellini and ask if he speaks French. No chance. Italian or English only and even the English with a Sicilian accent. Then I think: who speaks French around here?

Now, you guys would have shrugged and walked out, right? And you'd have missed something. But I'm Cholly Bloom, the sixth-sense man. And what stands just one block away at Twenty-sixth and Fifth? Delmonico's. And who runs Delmonico's? Why, Charlie Delmonico. And where does the Delmonico family come from? All right, Switzerland, but over there they speak all the languages and even though Charlie was born in the States I figure he probably has a little French.

So I wheel the Frenchie out of there and ten minutes later we are outside the most famous restaurant in the whole of the United States. You guys ever been in there? No? Well, it's something else. Polished mahogany, plum velvet, solid brass table lamps, seriously elegant. And expensive. More than I can afford. And up comes Charlie D. himself and he knows it. But that's the mark of a great restaurateur, right? Perfect manners, even to a tramp off the street. He bows and asks in what manner he can help. I explain that I have come across this Frenchie over from Paris and that he has a major problem with a letter but I cannot understand what it is.

Well, Mr. D. makes a polite enquiry of the Frenchman, in French, and the guy is at it again, going like a Gatling gun and producing his letter. I can't follow a word so I look around. Five tables away is Bet-a-Million Gates going through the menu from the date to the toothpick. Just beyond him is Diamond Jim Brady early dining with Lillian Russell, who has a décolletage to sink the SS *Majestic*. By the by, you know how Diamond Jim eats? I'd been told it but I never believed it; last night I saw it for real. He plants himself in his chair, measures an exact five inches, no more and no less, between his stomach and the table. Then he moves no more, but eats until his belly touches the table.

By this time Charlie D. has finished. He explains to me the Frenchie is a Mon-sewer Armand Dufour, a lawyer from Paris, who has come to New York on a mission of crucial importance. He has to deliver a letter from a dying woman to a certain Mr. Erik Muhlheim, who may or may not be a resident of New York.

He has tried every avenue and come up with a blank. At that point, so do I. Never heard of anybody of that name.

But Charlie is stroking his beard like he is thinking hard, then he says to me: "Mr. Bloom"—real formal—"have you heard of the E. M. Corporation?"

Now, I ask you, is the Pope Catholic? Of course I've heard of it. Incredibly rich, amazingly powerful and totally secretive. More shares of more pies quoted on the stock exchange than anyone barring J. Pierpont Morgan and no one is richer than J. P. So, not to be outdone, I say: Sure, based at the E. M. Tower on Park Row.

"Right," says Mr. D. "Well, it may just be that the extremely reclusive personage controlling the E. M. Corporation could be called Mr. Muhlheim." Now, when a guy like Charlie Delmonico says "It may just be," he means he has heard something but you never got it from him. Two minutes later we are back on the street, I hail a passing hansom and we are trotting downtown towards Park Row.

Now do you guys see why being a reporter can be the best job in the city? I started trying to help out a Frenchie with a problem and I am facing the chance of seeing the most elusive hermit in New York, the invisible man himself. Do I get to do this? Order up another pint of the golden brew, and I'll tell you.

We arrive at Park Row and drive up to the Tower. And boy, is it tall? It's enormous and its tip is damn near in the clouds. All the offices are closed, it's now dark outside but there is one lit-up lobby with a desk and a porter. So I ring the bell. He comes to enquire. I explain. He lets us into the lobby and calls someone on a private telephone. It must be an inside line because he does not ask for any operator. Then he speaks to someone and listens. Then he says we should leave the letter with him and it will be delivered.

Of course, I'm not having any of this. Tell the gentleman upstairs, says I, that Mon-sewer Dufour has come all the way from Paris and is charged to deliver the letter in person. The porter says something like that down the phone, then hands it to me. A voice says: "Who is this talking?" I say, "Charles Bloom, Esquire." And the voice says: "What is your mission here?"

Now, I'm not going to tell the voice that I am from the Hearst Press. I already have the impression that this is a recipe for going straight out the door. So I say I am the associate in New York City of Dufour Partners, notaries "of Paris, France." "And what is your mission here, Mr. Bloom?" asks the voice, sounding as if it came straight off the Newfoundland Banks. So I say again that we have to deliver a letter of signal importance into the hands personally of Mr. Erik Muhlheim. "There is no person of that name at this address" says the voice, "but if you leave the letter with the porter, I will ensure it reaches its destination."

Well, I'm not having any of this. It's a lie. I could even be speaking to Mr. Invisible for all I know. So I try a bluff. "Just tell Mr. Muhlheim," says I, "that the

letter comes from . . ." "Mme. Giry," says the lawyer.
"Mme. Giry," I repeat down the phone. "Wait," says
the voice. We wait again. Then he comes back on the
line. "Take the elevator to the thirty-ninth floor."

We do that. You guys ever been up thirty-nine
floors? No? Well, it's an experience. Locked in a cage,
the machinery clanking all around you, and you're going up into the sky. And it sways. Eventually the cage
stops, I pull the grille to one side and we step out.
There's a fellow there, the voice. "I am Mr. Darius,"
he says. "Follow me."

He takes us into a long, paneled room with a boardroom table set with silver pieces. Clearly this is where
the deals are struck, the rivals crushed, the weak
bought out, the millions made. It's elegant, Old World
style. There are oil paintings on the walls and I notice
one at the far end, higher than the rest. A guy in a
wide-brimmed hat, mustache, lace collar, smiling.
"May I see the letter?" says Darius, fixing me with a
stare like a cobra sizing up a muskrat for lunch. Okay,
I've never seen a cobra or a muskrat, but I can imagine.
I nod to Dufour and he puts the letter on the polished
table between him and Darius. There is something
strange about this man that sends the hairs on my neck
straight up. He's all in black: black frock coat, white
shirt, black tie. Face as white as the shirt, thin, narrow.
Black hair and jet-black eyes that glitter but do not
blink. I said cobra? Cobra will do just fine.

Now, listen up, guys, 'cause this is important. I feel
the need for a cigarette, so I light up. Mistake, bad

move. When the match sputters Darius comes round on me like a knife out of a sheath. "No naked flame, if you please," he snaps. "Extinguish the cigarette."

Now, I am still standing at the end of the table, near the corner door. Behind me there is a half-moon table against the wall with a silver bowl on it. I walk to it to stub out the butt. Behind the silver bowl is a vast silver salver, one edge on the table and the other on the wall so it is tilted at an angle. Just as I stub the cigarette I glance into the salver, which is like a mirror. At the far end of the room, high on the wall, the oil painting of the smiling guy has changed. A face is there, wide-brimmed hat, yes. But beneath that hat is a visage to scare the Rough Riders right out of their saddles.

Under the hat is a kind of mask covering three-quarters of where the face should be. Just showing half of a crooked gash of a mouth. And behind the mask, two eyes boring into me like drills. I let out a yell and turn around, pointing up at the picture on the wall. "Who the hell's that?" I yell.

"*The Laughing Cavalier* by Frans Hals," says Darius. "Not the original, I fear, which is in London, but a very fine copy."

And sure enough, the laughing guy is back, mustache, lace and all. But I am not crazy, I know what I saw. Anyway, Darius reaches out and takes the letter. "You have my assurance," he says, "that within an hour Mr. Muhlheim will have his letter." Then he says the same thing in French to Dufour. The lawyer nods.

If he is satisfied there is nothing more I can do. We turn towards the door. Before I can get there, Darius says: "By the way, Mr. Bloom, from which newspaper do you come?" Voice like razor blades. "*New York American.*" I mumble. Then we are gone. Back down to the street, into a cab, back to Broadway. I drop the Frenchie off where he wants to go and head for the city desk. I have a story, right?

Wrong. The night editor looks up, and says, "Cholly, you're drunk." "I'm whaaaat? I haven't touched a drop," says I. I tell him my adventure of the evening. Start to finish. What a story, eh? He will have none of it. "Okay," he says, "you found a French lawyer with a letter to deliver and you helped him deliver it. Big deal. But no ghosts. I just had a call from the president of the E. M. Corporation, a certain Mr. Darius. He says you called this evening, delivered a letter to him personally, lost your head and started shouting about apparitions in the walls. He is grateful for the letter, but threatens to sue if you start casting slurs on his corporation. By the way, the bulls just picked up the Central Park murderer. Caught him in the act. Get down there and help out."

So not a word was printed. But I tell you guys, I am not crazy and I was not drunk. I really saw that face in the wall. Hey, you are drinking with the only guy in New York who ever actually saw the Phantom of Manhattan.

FIVE

THE TRANCE OF DARIUS

I can feel the smoke entering me, soft, seductive smoke. Behind closed eyes I can leave this shoddy, shabby slum and walk alone through the gates of perception into the domain of Him whom I serve.

The smoke clears . . . the long passage floored and walled in solid gold. Oh, the pleasure of the gold. To touch, to caress, to feel, to own. And to bring it to Him, the god of gold, the only true deity.

Since the Barbary Coast where I first found Him, I a foul catamite elevated to a higher calling, seeking always more gold to bring Him and the smoke to take me to his presence . . .

I walk forward into the great golden chamber where

the smelters roar and the golden torrents run fresh and endless from their spigots . . . More smoke, the smoke of the smelters mingling with that in my mouth, my throat, my blood, my brain. And out of that smoke He will speak to me as ever. . . .

He will listen to me, advise and counsel me and as always He will be right. . . . He is here now, I can feel his presence. . . . "Master, great God Mammon, I am on my knees before you. I have served you as best I have been able these many years and have brought to your throne my earthly employer and all his stupendous wealth. I beg you to hear me, for I need your advice and help."

"I hear you, Servant. What is your trouble?"

"That man whom I serve here below . . . something seems to have entered him that I cannot comprehend."

"Explain."

"Ever since I have known him, ever since I first cast my eyes on that hideous face, he has had but one obsession. Which I have encouraged and fostered at every stage. In a world that he perceives as being uniformly hostile to him, he has only ever wanted to succeed. It was I who channeled that obsession into the making of money and ever more money and thus brought him to your service. Is it not so?"

"You have done brilliantly, Servant. Every day his wealth increases and you ensure that it is dedicated to my service."

"But recently, Master, he has increasingly become obsessed with another concern. Time-wasting but worse, much worse, a waste of money. He thinks only of opera. There is no profit in opera."

"This I know. A fruitless irrelevance. How much of his fortune does he devote to this fetish?"

"So far, but a tiny fraction. My fear is that it distracts him from dedication to the increase of your empire of gold."

"Does he cease to make money?"

"On the contrary. In that area things are as they have always been. The original ideas, the great strategies, the extraordinary ingenuity which sometimes seems to me like a second sight, these he still has. I still preside over the meetings in the boardroom. It is I who, for the world, conduct the great takeovers, construct an ever bigger empire of mergers and investments. It is I who destroy the weak and the helpless, rejoicing in their pleas. It is I who raise the rents in the slum tenements, order the clearances of the homes and schools for factories and marshaling yards. It is I who suborn and bribe the city officials to ensure their complaisance. It is I who sign the purchase orders for great stakes of shares and blocks of stock in the rising industries across the country. But always the instructions are his, the campaign planned by him, the things I must do and say devised by him."

"And is his judgment starting to fail him?"

"No, Master. It is as faultless as ever. The stock exchange is agape at his audacity and foresight, even though they think it is mine."

"Then what is the problem, Servant?"

"I am wondering, Master, if the moment has come for him to depart and for me to inherit."

"Servant, you have done brilliantly, but because you have also followed my orders. You are talented, it is true, and you have always known this, and loyal only to me. But Erik Muhlheim is more. Rarely does one come across a true genius in the matter of gold. He is such a one, and more besides. Inspired only by hatred of Man, guided by you in my service, he is not simply a wealth-creating genius but immune to scruple, principle, mercy, pity, compassion, and most important of all, like you immune to love. A human tool to dream of. One day his moment will indeed come and I may order you to end his life. So that you may inherit, of course. "All the kingdoms of the world" was the phrase I used once, to Another. To you, all the financial empire of America. Have I deceived you so far?"

"Never, Master."

"And have you betrayed me?"

"Never, Master."

"Then so be it. Let it continue a while. Tell me more of this new obsession, and the why of it."

"His library shelves have always been loaded with the works of opera and books concerning it. But when I arranged that he could never have a private box, screened by curtains to hide his face, at the Metropolitan he seemed to lose interest. Now he has invested millions in a rival opera house."

"So far he has always recouped his investments and more."

"True, but this venture is a certain loss-maker, even though such losses must be under one percent of his total wealth. And there is more. His mood has changed."

"Why?"

"I do not know, Master. Save that it began after the arrival of a mysterious letter from Paris where he once lived."

"Tell me."

"Two men came. One a shoddy little reporter from a New York newspaper, but he was only the guide. The other was a lawyer from France. He had a letter. I would have opened it but he was watching me. When they had gone he came down and took the letter. He sat and read it at the boardroom table. I pretended to leave but watched through a chink in the door. When he rose he seemed changed."

"And since then?"

"Before that he was simply the sleeping partner behind a man called Hammerstein, builder and moving spirit behind the new opera house. Hammerstein is wealthy but not to compare. It was Muhlheim who pledged enough to bring the opera house to completion.

"But since the letter he has become involved to a greater degree. He had already despatched Hammerstein to Paris with a torrent of money to persuade a singer called Dame Nellie Melba to come to New York and star in the New Year. Now he has sent a frantic message to Paris ordering Hammerstein to secure yet another prima donna, the great rival of Melba, a French singer called Christine de Chagny.

"He has involved himself in the artistic choices, changing the inaugural opera from one by Bellini to another, insisting on a different cast. But most of all, he spends every night furiously writing. . . ."

"Writing what?"

"Music, Master. I hear him in the penthouse above. Each morning there are fresh sheaves of music. In the small hours I hear the tones of that organ he has installed in his drawing room. I am tone-deaf; it means nothing to me, a meaningless noise. But he is composing something up there and I believe it is his own opera. Just yesterday he commissioned the fastest packet on the East Coast to take the so-far completed part of the work and rush it over to Paris. What am I to do?"

"It is all madness, my servant, but relatively harmless. Has he invested more money in this wretched opera house?"

"No, Master, but I worry for my inheritance. Long ago he pledged to me that should anything ever happen to him I should inherit his entire empire, his hundreds of millions of dollars, and thus continue to dedicate them to your service. Now I fear he may be changing his mind. He could leave everything he has to some kind of foundation dedicated to his wretched obsession with opera."

"Foolish servant. You are his adoptive son, his inheritor, his successor, the one destined to take over his empire of gold and power. Has he not promised you? More to the point, have I not promised you? And can I be defeated?"

"No, Master, you are supreme, the only god."

"Then calm yourself. But on reflection let me tell you this. Not advice, but a flat order. If ever you should perceive a real threat to your inheritance of everything he has—his money, his gold, his power, his kingdom— then you will destroy that threat without mercy or delay. Do I make myself plain?"

"Perfectly, my Master. And thank you. I have your orders."

SIX

THE COLUMN OF GAYLORD SPRIGGS

OPERA CRITIC, *THE NEW YORK TIMES*,
NOVEMBER 1906

To opera-lovers of New York City and even those within range of our great metropolis I come bearing tidings of good news. War has broken out.

No, not a resumption of that Spanish-American War in which our President Teddy Roosevelt so distinguished himself some years ago at San Juan Hill, but a war within the world of opera in our city. And why should such a war be of good news? Because the troops will be the finest voices on the planet today, the ammunition will be money of the sort of which most of us can only dream and the beneficiaries will be those who love superlative opera.

But let me, in the words of the King of Hearts in

Alice in Wonderland—and New York opera is starting to resemble Lewis Carroll's recent fantasy—begin at the beginning. Devotees will know that in October 1883 the Metropolitan Opera opened its doors to an inaugural rendition of Gounod's *Faust* and thus planted New York firmly into a world setting, along with Covent Garden and La Scala.

But why was such a magnificent home for opera, seating no less than 3,700 in the world's largest auditorium for opera, open at all? Why, pique coupled with money, a powerful combination. The richest and most grand of the new aristocracy of this city were deeply offended that they could not secure private and guaranteed boxes at the old Academy of Music on Fourteenth Street, now deceased.

So they clubbed together, dug deep and now regularly enjoy their opera in the style and comfort to which the members of Mrs. Astor's Four Hundred list are well accustomed. And what glories the Met has brought us over the years and continues to do today under the inspired leadership of Mr. Heinrich Conreid. But did I say "war?" I did. For now a new Lochinvar rides over the horizon to challenge the Met with a galaxy of names to take the breath away.

After an earlier abortive attempt to open an opera house of his own, tobacco millionaire and theater designer/builder Oscar Hammerstein has just completed the richly ornate Manhattan Opera House on West Thirty-fourth Street. Smaller, it is true, but with luxurious accoutrements, lush seating and superb acoustics it bids to rival the Met by pitting quality against quantity. But where is this quality to come from? Why, no less than Dame Nellie Melba herself.

Yes, this is the first good news from the opera war. Dame Nellie, who has always and steadfastly refused to cross the Atlantic, has agreed to come—and for a fee that takes the breath away. My highly reliable source in Paris tells me this is the story behind the story.

For a month past Mr. Hammerstein has been paying court to the Australian diva in her residence at Garnier's Grand Hotel, built by that same genius who built the Paris Opera House where Dame Nellie has so often performed. At first she refused. He offered $1,500 a night—imagine it! Still she refused. He shouted through her bathroom keyhole, raising the fee yet again. To $2,500 a night. Unbelievable. Then $3,000 a night, in a house where the chorus is paid $15 a week or $3 per show.

He finally invaded her private salon at the Grand and began throwing thousand-franc notes all over the floor. Despite her protests he continued before storming out. When Dame Nellie finally counted all the money, he had left 100,000 French francs, or $20,000 scattered on the Persian carpet. I am informed that this has now been lodged with Rothschilds in the rue Lafitte, but the Dame's defenses are down. She has agreed to come. After all, she was once an Australian farmer's wife and can surely recognize a sheep being fleeced.

If this were all, it would be enough to cause heart attacks at Broadway and Thirty-ninth where Mr. Conreid holds sway. But there is more. For Mr. Hammer-stein had engaged none other than Alessandro Gonci, only possible rival in quality and fame to the already immortal Enrico Caruso, to sing the tenor lead on December third at the inaugural performance. To support Signor Gonci, other great names like Amadeo Bassi and Charles Dalmores are on the menu, with baritones Mario Ancona and Maurice Renaud and a further soprano Emma Calvé.

This alone would be enough to set New York by the ears. But there is even more. Long ears and sharp tongues have maintained for some time that even Mr. Hammerstein's wealth could not permit such amazing extravagance. There must be a secret Croesus behind him, calling the shots, pulling the strings and perforce paying the bills. But who is this invisible paymaster, this phantom of Manhattan? Whoever he is, he has now surely exceeded himself in his attempts to spoil us. For if there is one name that acts upon Nellie Melba like a red rag to a bull it is that of her only rival, the younger and stunningly beautiful French aristocrat Christine de Chagny, known throughout Italy as La Divina.

What, I hear you cry, she cannot be coming too? But she is. And herein lies a mystery and a double mystery.

The first is that like Dame Nellie Melba, La Divina has always declined to cross the Atlantic, calculating that such an expedition would occupy too much time and trouble. For this reason the Met has never been favored by either of them. Yet while Dame Nellie has clearly been seduced by the astronomical sums poured upon her by Mr. Hammerstein, Vicomtesse de Chagny is noted for her complete immunity to the lure of the dollar, no matter what the quantity.

If a torrent of dollars was the argument which prevailed upon the Australian Dame, what was the argument that convinced the French aristocrat? This we simply do not know—as yet.

Our second mystery concerns a sudden change in the artistic calendar of the new Manhattan Opera House. Before departing for Paris on his quest for the world's most famous divas, Mr. Hammerstein had announced that the inaugural opera on December third would be Bellini's *I Puritani*.

The construction of sets had already begun, programs sent to the printers. Now I hear that the invisible paymaster has insisted there will be a change. Gone is *I Puritani*. In its place the Manhattan will inaugurate with a completely new opera by an unknown and even *anonymous* composer. It is an awesome risk, utterly unheard-of. It is all too amazing.

Of the two prima donnas, who will star in this unknown new work? They cannot both do so. Who will arrive first? Which one will sing with Gonci to the fierce baton of yet another star, conductor Cleofonte Campanini? They cannot both do so. How will the Metropolitan fight back with its highly risky choice of *Salome* as the season-starter? What is the name of this new, untried work that the Manhattan insists upon for its inaugural? Will it prove a complete flop?

There are enough hotels in New York of the finest quality to permit the two prima donnas not to share the same roof, but what about the liners? France has two stars, *La Savoie* and *La Lorraine*. They will simply have to have one each. Oh, opera-lovers, what a winter to be alive!!

SEVEN

THE
LESSON of
PIERRE DE CHAGNY

SS *LORRAINE*, LONG ISLAND SOUND,
NOVEMBER 28, 1906

"Well, what's it going to be today, young Pierre? Latin, I think."

"Oh, do we have to, Father Joe? We'll be coming into New York Harbor soon. The captain told Mama over breakfast."

"But at the moment we are still passing Long Island and an empty coast it is. Nothing to see but mist and sand. A fine moment to kill some time with Caesar's Gallic War. Open your book where we left off."

"Is it important, Father Joe?"

"It certainly is."

"But why should Caesar invading England be important?"

"Well, if you were a Roman legionary heading into an unknown land of wild savages you'd have thought so. And if you were an ancient Briton with the eagles of Rome marching up the beach you'd have thought so too."

"But I'm not a Roman soldier and certainly not an ancient Briton. I'm a modern Frenchman."

"With whom I am charged, heaven save us, to try and give a good education, academic and moral. So, Caesar's first invasion of the island he only knew as Britannia. Start at the top of the page."

" '*Accidit ut eadem nocte luna esset plena.*' "

"Good. Translate."

" 'It fell . . . *nocte* means 'night' . . . night fell?' "

"No, night did not fall. It had already fallen. He was looking up at the sky. And *accidit* means 'it befell' or 'happened.' Start again."

" 'It happened that on the same night . . . er . . . the moon was full?' "

"Precisely. Now put it into better English."

" 'It happened that on the same night there was a full moon.' "

"There was indeed. You're lucky with Caesar. He was a soldier and he wrote in clear soldier's language. When we get on to Ovid, Horace, Juvenal and Virgil there will be some real brainteasers. Why did he say *esset* and not *erat*?"

"Subjunctive tense?"

"Well done. An element of doubt. It might not have been a full moon but by chance it was. So, the subjunctive. He was lucky with the moon."

"Why, Father Joe?"

"Because, lad, he was invading a foreign land in the dark. No powerful searchlights in those days. No lighthouses to keep you off the rocks. He needed to find a flat, shingly beach between the cliffs. So, the moonlight was a help."

"Did he invade Ireland too?"

"He did not. Old Hibernia remained inviolate for another twelve hundred years, long after St. Patrick brought us Christianity. And then it was not the Romans but the British. And you're a cunning dog, trying to draw me away from Caesar's Gallic War."

"But can't we talk about Ireland, Father Joe? I have seen most of Europe now, but never Ireland."

"Oh, why not? Caesar can make his landfall at Pevensey Bay tomorrow. What do you want to know?"

"Did you come from a rich family? Did your parents have a fine house and broad estates like mine?"

"Indeed they did not. For most of the great estates are owned by the English or the Anglo-Irish. But the Kilfoyles go back before the conquest. And mine were just poor farming people."

"Are most of the Irish poor?"

"Well, certainly the people of the countryside do not have any silver spoons. Most are tenant farmers in a small way, scraping a living from the land. My people are like that. I came from a small farm outside the town of Mullingar. My father tilled the land from dawn till dusk. There were nine of us in the brood; I was the second-born son and we lived mostly on potatoes mixed with milk from our two cows and beets from the fields."

"But you got an education, Father Joe?"

"Of course I did. Ireland may be poor, but she is steeped in saints and scholars, poets and soldiers, and now a few priests. But the Irish are concerned with the love of God and education, in that order. So we all went to the village school, which was run by the fathers. Three miles away and walking barefoot. All the way, each way. Summer evenings until after dark and all the holidays we helped our Da on the farm. Then homework in the light of a single candle until we fell asleep, five of us in one bunk and the four small ones tucked in with our parents."

"*Mon Dieu*, did you not have ten bedrooms?"

"Listen, young lad, your bedroom at the château is bigger than was the entire farmhouse. You're luckier than you know."

"You have traveled a long way since then, Father Joe."

"Oh, that I have, and I wonder daily why the Lord favored me in such a way."

"But you still got an education."

"Yes, and a good one. Driven into us by a combination of patience, love and the strap. Reading and writing, sums and Latin, history but not much geography, for the fathers had never been anywhere and it was presumed we would never do so either."

"Why did you decide to become a priest, Father Joe?"

"Well, we had mass every morning before lessons, and of course on Sundays as a family. I became an altar boy and something about the mass got into me. I used to look at the great wooden figure above the altar and think that if He had done that for me, then perhaps I ought to serve Him as best I could. I was good at school and when I was about to leave I asked if there was any chance of being sent to train for the priesthood.

"Well, I knew my older brother would take over the farm one day and I would certainly be one less mouth to feed. And I was lucky. I was sent into Mullingar for an interview, with a note from Father Gabriel at the school, and they accepted me for the seminary at Kildare. Miles away. A major adventure."

"But now you are with us in Paris and London, St. Petersburg and Berlin."

"Yes, but that is now. When I was fifteen the coach to Kildare was a big adventure. So I was tested again and accepted, and studied for years until the time came for ordination. There was quite a group of us in my class and the Cardinal Archbishop himself came from Dublin to ordain us all. When it was over I thought to go and spend my life as a humble parish priest somewhere in the West, a forgotten parish in Connaught perhaps. And I would have accepted that with a glad heart.

"But I was called back by the principal. He was with another man whom I did not know. It turned out he was Bishop Delaney of Clontarf and he needed a private secretary. They said I had a good clear hand for the writing and would I like the post? Well, it was almost too good to be true. I was twenty-one and they were inviting me to live in a bishop's palace and be secretary to a man responsible for a whole see.

"So I went with Bishop Delaney, a good and holy man, and spent five years at Clontarf and learned many things."

"Why did you not stay there, Father Joe?"

"I thought I would, or at least until the Church found other work for me. A parish in Dublin perhaps, or Cork or Waterford. But then chance struck again. Ten years ago the Papal Nuncio, the Pope's ambassador to the whole of Britain, came from London to tour his Irish provinces and spent three days at Clontarf. He had a retinue, did Cardinal Massini, and one of them was Monsignor Eamonn Byrne from the Irish College in Rome. We found ourselves thrown together quite a bit and got along well. We discovered we were born only ten miles apart, though he was several years older.

"The cardinal went on his way and I thought no more about it. Four weeks later a letter arrived from the principal of the Irish College offering me a place. Bishop Delaney said he was sorry to see me go but gave me his blessing and urged me to take the chance. So I packed my single bag and took the train to Dublin. I thought that was big, until the ferry and another train brought me to London. Sure I had never seen such a place nor thought any city could be so big and grand.

"Then there was a ferry to France and another train, this time to Paris. Another amazing sight; I could hardly believe what I was seeing. The last train brought me through the Alps and down to Rome itself."

"Were you surprised by Rome?"

"Amazed and overawed. Here was the Vatican City itself, the Sistine Chapel, the Basilica of St. Peter. . . . I stood in the crowd and looked up at the balcony and took the *Urbi et Orbi* blessing from His Holiness himself. And I wondered how a boy from a potato patch outside Mullingar could ever have come so far and been so privileged. So I wrote home to my parents, telling them everything, and they took the letter round the whole village and showed it to everyone and they became celebrities themselves."

"But why do you now live with us, Father Joe?"

"Another coincidence, Pierre. Six years ago your mama came to sing in Rome. I know nothing of opera but by chance a member of the cast, an Irishman, collapsed with a heart attack in the wings. Someone was sent running to ask for a priest and I was on duty that night. There was nothing I could do for the poor man but give him the Last Rites, but he had been carried to your mama's dressing room at her insistence. That was where I met her. She was very distressed. I tried to comfort her by explaining that God is never malign, even when He takes back one of his children to Himself. I had made it my business to master Italian and French, so we spoke in French. It seemed to surprise her that someone should speak both, plus English and Gaelic.

"She also had problems for other reasons. Her career was taking her all over Europe, from Russia to Spain, from London to Vienna. Your father needed to spend more time with his estates in Normandy. You were over six and running wild, your education constantly interrupted by the traveling, but too young for boarding school and anyway she did not wish to be parted from you. I suggested she might engage a resident tutor to travel with her everywhere. She was thinking it over when I left to return to the college and resume my studies.

"Her engagement was for a week, and on the day before she left I was summoned to the office of the principal, and there she was. Clearly she had made quite an impression. She wished me to become your tutor, both for formal education, moral guidance and a bit of manly control thrown in. I was dumbfounded and tried to decline.

"But the principal would have none of it and he made it a flat order. As obedience is one of the vows, the die was cast. And as you know I have been with you ever since, trying to shove some knowledge into that head of yours and keep you from becoming a complete barbarian."

"Do you regret it, Father Joe?"

"No, I do not. For your father is a fine man, better than you know, and your mama is a great lady with an extraordinary God-given talent. I live and eat too well, of course, and must say constant penance for this life of luxury, but I have seen amazing things: cities to take the breath away, paintings and art galleries that are the stuff of legend, operas to make you cry, and me a boy from the potato patch!"

"I'm glad Mama chose you, Father Joe."

"Well, thank you for that, but you won't be when we start into Caesar's Gallic War again. Which ought to be now, but here comes your mother. Stand up, lad!"

"What are you two doing in here? We have turned into the harbor, the sun has come out and burned off the mist and from the bow you can see all of New York moving towards us. Wrap up warm and come to look. For this is one of the greatest sights of the world and if we depart in darkness you will never see it again."

"Very good, my lady, we are on our way. Looks as if you are lucky once again, Pierre. No more Caesar today."

"Father Joe?"

"Mmm?"

"Will there be great adventures in New York?"

"More than enough, for the captain has told me there is a huge civic reception awaiting at the docking pier. We'll be staying at the Waldorf-Astoria, one of the biggest and most famous hotels in the world. In five days your mama will open a brand-new opera house and star nightly for a week. In that time I think we'll be able to explore a little, see the sights, ride the new elevated train—I have read all about it in a book I bought in Le Havre. . . .

"Well, now, will you look at that, Pierre? Is it not a fantastic sight? Liners and tugs, freighters and tramps, schooners and paddlers; how on earth do they not bang into each other? And there she is, look, over to the left. The Lady with the Lamp herself, the Statue of Liberty. Ah, Pierre, if you only knew how many wretched people, fleeing from the Old World, have seen her coming out of the mist and known they were starting a new life. Millions of them, including my own fellow countrymen and -women. For since the Great Famine fifty years ago half of Ireland has moved to New York, crammed like cattle into the steerage holds, coming on deck in the freezing cold of morning to watch the city move across the water and pray they would be allowed in.

"Since then many of them have moved inland, even as far as the coast of California to help create a new nation. But many are still here in New York, the Irish-Americans, more in this city alone than in all of Dublin, Cork, and Belfast combined. So, I'll be feeling quite at home here, my lad. I'll even be able to get a pint of good Irish stout, which I have not found for many years.

"Yes, New York will indeed be for all of us a great adventure and who knows what will happen to us here? God alone knows but He will not tell us. So we must find out for ourselves. Now, time to go and change for the civic reception. Young Meg will stay with your mama; you stick close by me all the way to the hotel."

"Okay, Father Joe. That's what the Americans say. Okay. I read it in a book. And will you look after me in New York?"

"Of course, lad. Do I not always, when your papa is not here? Now run along. Best suit and best manners."

EIGHT

THE DISPATCH OF BERNARD SMITH

SHIPPING CORRESPONDENT, *NEW YORK AMERICAN*,
NOVEMBER 29, 1906

Further proof was offered, if further proof was even needed, that the great harbor of New York has become the greatest magnet in the world for the reception of the finest and most luxurious liners our earth has ever seen.

Just ten years ago barely more than three luxury liners plied the North Atlantic route from Europe to the New World. The voyage was hard and most travelers favored the summer months. Today our tugs and lightermen are spoiled for choice.

The British Inman Line now has a regular schedule with her *City of Paris*. Cunards match their rivals with the new *Campania* and *Lucania* while the White Star

Line fight back with *Majestic* and *Teutonic*. All these Britishers are fighting for the privilege of carrying the rich and famous from Europe to experience the hospitality of our great city.

Yesterday it was the turn of the Compagnie Générale Transatlantique out of Le Havre, France, to send the jewel of their crown, *La Lorraine*, sister ship of the equally sumptuous *La Savoie* to take up her reserved berth on the Hudson River. Nor were her passengers confined to the cream of the high society of France; the *Lorraine* brought us all an extra and very special prize.

Small wonder that from the breakfast hour, even before the French ship was clear of the Roads and rounding the tip of Battery Point, a host of private broughams and hansoms was beginning to choke Canal Street and Morton Street as sightseers from the mansions uptown sought a place from which to applaud our guest, New York style.

And who was she? Why, none other than Christine, Vicomtesse de Chagny, deemed by many to be the greatest opera soprano in the world—but don't tell Dame Nellie Melba, who is due in ten days!

The French Line's Pier 42 was decked overall with bunting and *tricolore* flags as the sun came out and the mist lifted to reveal the *Lorraine*, with her tugs fussing about her, easing herself stern first into her berth on the Hudson.

Space was at a premium for the craning crowds as the *Lorraine* greeted us with three great whoops from her foghorn and smaller vessels up and down the river responded in kind. At the head of the pier was the podium, hung with French flags and Old Glory, where Mayor George B. McClellan would offer Mme. de Chagny a formal welcome to New York just five days before she will star in the inaugural opera at the new Manhattan Opera House.

Grouped around the base of the podium was a sea of shining top hats and waving bonnets as half of New York society waited for a glimpse of the incoming star. From neighboring piers dockhands and stevedores who must surely never have heard of opera house or soprano clambered up cranes to satisfy their curiosity. Before the *Lorraine* had cast her first hawser down to the pier, every structure along the quay was black with humanity. French Line staff rolled out a long red carpet from the dais to the base of the gangway as soon as the latter was in place.

Customs men scurried up the gangway to complete the necessary formalities for the diva and her entourage in the privacy of her stateroom even as, with due pomp and circumstance, the mayor arrived at the pierhead accompanied by a blue-coated squad of New York's Finest. He and the bosses of City Hall and Tammany Hall who had come with him were escorted through the throng to mount the podium while a police band struck up "The Star-Spangled Banner." All hats were doffed as the mayor and city dignitaries took their places on the dais, facing down the pier to the lower end of the gangway.

For myself, I had avoided the ground-level press enclosure to occupy a window on the second floor of a warehouse right on the pierhead and from here I could look out upon the entire scene, the better to describe to readers of the *American* just what happened.

Aboard the *Lorraine* herself the first-class passengers stared down from the upper decks, having themselves a grandstand view but prevented from disembarking until the civic welcome was over. In the lower portholes I could see the faces of the steerage-class passengers peering out and up to see what was going on.

At a few minutes before ten there was a hubbub on the *Lorraine* as the captain and a group of officers escorted a single figure towards the head of the gangway. After cordial farewells to her French compatriots, Madame de Chagny began her journey down the gangway to her first-ever contact with American soil. Waiting to greet her was Mr. Oscar Hammerstein, the impresario who owns and runs the Manhattan Opera and whose tenacity of purpose has succeeded in enticing both the vicomtesse and Dame Nellie across the Atlantic in winter to sing for us.

With an Old World gesture seen with increasing rarity in our society, he bowed and kissed her extended hand. There was a loud "Ooooooh" and some whistles from the workers clinging to the surrounding derricks but the mood was joyful rather than mocking and a round of applause greeted the gesture—it came from the ranks of the silk top hats grouped around the podium.

Reaching the red carpet Mme. de Chagny turned and, on the arm of Mr. Hammerstein, proceeded the length of the quay towards the dais. As she did so, and with a flair that would certainly put her in the running for Mayor McClellan's job, she waved and flashed a beaming smile at the dockhands atop the packing-crates and hanging from the girders of the cranes. They replied with even more whistles, this time of great appreciation. As none of them will ever hear her sing, this gesture went down extremely well.

Through powerful glasses I could bring the lady into focus from my upper window. At thirty-two she is very beautiful, trim and petite. Opera-lovers have been known to wonder how such a magnificent voice could be contained in such a lissome frame. She wore from shoulder to ankles—for despite the sun the temperature was just above zero—a tight-waisted and befrogged coat in burgundy velvet, trimmed with mink at throat, cuffs and hem, with a circular Cossack-style hat of the same fur. Her hair was tucked into a neat chignon behind her head. The ladies of fashion of New York City will have to look to their laurels when this lady saunters down Peacock Alley.

Behind her I could see her remarkably small and nonfussy entourage descending the gangway: her personal maid and former colleague Mlle. Giry, two male secretaries to handle her correspondence and traveling arrangements, her son, Pierre, a handsome boy of twelve, and his traveling tutor, an Irish priest in black soutane and broad-brimmed hat, youthful himself, with a wide and open grin.

As the lady was helped up to the podium Mayor McClellan shook her hand, American style, and launched into his formal welcome, something he will have to repeat in ten days' time for the Australian Dame Nellie Melba. But if there were any fears that Mme. de Chagny might not understand what was being said, these were soon dispelled. She needed no translation and indeed when the mayor had finished she stepped to the front of the dais and thanked us all most prettily in fluent English with a delightful French accent.

What she had to say was both surprising and flattering. After her thanks to the mayor and the city for a most touching reception, she confirmed that she had come to sing for one week only in the inaugural opera at the Manhattan Opera House and that the work in question would be an entirely new opera, never heard before, by an unknown American composer.

Then she revealed new details. The story was set in the American Civil War and entitled *The Angel of Shiloh*, concerning the struggle between love and duty besetting a Southern belle in love with a Union officer. She would sing the role of Eugenie Delarue. She added that she had seen the libretto and score in Paris in manuscript form, and it was the sheer beauty of the work that had caused her to change her itinerary and cross the Atlantic. Clearly her implication was that money had played no part in her decision, a poke in the eye for Dame Nellie Melba. Again the working men on the cranes around the pier, silent while she spoke, let out a prolonged cheer and many whistles, which would have been ill-mannered if they were not so obviously admiring. Again she waved at them and turned to descend the steps on the other side in order to board her waiting coach.

At this point, in a hitherto carefully staged and flaw-less ceremony, two things happened which were em-phatically not on the foreseen scenario. The first was puzzling and seen by few; the second caused a roar of amusement.

For some reason I let my glance stray from the dais below me while she was speaking and saw, standing on the roof of a great warehouse directly opposite mine, a strange figure. It was of a man, standing quite motion-less and staring down. He wore a broad-brimmed hat and was otherwise wrapped in a flowing cloak that flapped about him in the wind. There was something strange and vaguely sinister about the lone figure, standing high above us, looking down on the lady from France as she spoke. How did he get up there unseen? What was he doing? Why was he not with the rest of the crowd?

I adjusted my spyglass for a new focus; he must have seen the sun glint on the lenses for he suddenly looked up and stared straight back at me. Then I saw that he wore a mask over his face and through the eyeholes it seemed as if he gazed fiercely at me for a couple of seconds. I heard a few shouts from the dockhands clinging still to the cold steel of the derricks, and saw pointing fingers. But by the time those below started to look up, he was gone, with a speed that defies explanation. One second he was there, the next the skyline was empty. He had vanished as if he had never been.

Seconds later the small chill this apparition might have created was dispelled by a roar of applause and laughter from below. Mme. de Chagny had emerged from the rear of the raised speaking dais and was approaching the liveried brougham prepared for her by Mr. Hammerstein. The mayor and the city fathers were a few steps behind. All saw that between their guest and her carriage, beyond the range of the red carpet, lay a large pool of half-melted slush, evidently left over from yesterday's snowfall.

A man's stout boots would have made short shrift of it, but the French aristocrat's dainty shoes? New York City's government stood and stared in dismay but helpless. Then I saw a young man vault over the barrier that surrounded the press enclosure. He was wearing a coat of his own but carried over his arm something else which was soon revealed as a large evening cape. This he swung in an arc so that it landed right over the slush between the opera star and the open door of her brougham. The lady flashed a brilliant smile, stepped onto the cape and in two seconds was inside her carriage with the coachman closing the door.

The young man picked up his soaking and muddied cape and exchanged a few words with the face framed in the window before the coach rattled away. Mayor McClellan gave the young man a grateful pat on the back and as he turned I perceived it was none other than a young colleague of mine on this very newspaper.

All's well, as the saying goes, that ends well and the welcome by New York to the lady from Paris ended extremely well. Now she is ensconced in the finest suite at the Waldorf-Astoria with five days of rehearsals and voice protecting before her no doubt triumphant debut at the Manhattan Opera House on December third.

Meanwhile I suspect that a certain young colleague of mine from the city desk will be explaining to one and all that the spirit of Raleigh is not entirely dead!!

NINE

THE OFFER OF CHOLLY BLOOM

LOUIE'S BAR, FIFTH AVENUE AT TWENTY-EIGHTH STREET, NEW YORK CITY, NOVEMBER 29, 1906

Did I ever get around to telling you guys that being a reporter in New York is the greatest job in the world? I did? Well, forgive me, but I'm going to say it again. Anyway, you have to forgive me, 'cause I'm buying. Barney, could we have a round of beers?

Mind you, you got to show flair, energy and ingenuity amounting almost to genius and that is why I am saying this job has got it all. I mean, take yesterday. Were any of you at Pier 42 yesterday morning? You should have been. What a spectacle, what an event. You read this morning's coverage in the *American*? Good for you, Harry, at least someone here reads a decent newspaper even if you do work for the *Post*.

Now, I have to say it wasn't really my job. Our shipping man was there to give complete coverage. But I had nothing assigned for the morning so I figured I'd go anyway and, boy, did I get a break. Now, the rest of you guys would have spent the morning in bed. That's what I mean by energy; you got to be out and about to get life's lucky breaks. Where was I? Oh, yes.

Someone told me the French liner *Lorraine* was docking at Pier 42 and bringing in this French singer lady who I had never heard of but who is very big bagels in the opera world. Mme. Christine de Chagny. Now, I have never been to an opera in my life but I thought, what the hell? She's a big star, no one can get near her for an interview, so I'll go and have a look anyway. Besides, the last time I tried to help a Frenchie out of a jam I damn near got a major scoop and I would have done except that our city editor is a four-star schlemiel. I told you about that? The weird incident at the E. M. Tower. Well, listen up, this gets weirder. Would I lie? Is the Mufti a Moslem?

I went down to the pier just after nine. The *Lorraine* was coming in stern first. Plenty of time, these dockings always take forever. So I wave my pass at the bulls and saunter over to the press enclosure. Clearly it is as well I showed up. This is obviously going to be a major civic reception—Mayor McClellan, city fathers, Tammany Hall, the lot. I know the whole shindig will be covered by the docks correspondent, whom I spot after a while in an upper window with a better view.

Well, they play the anthems and this French lady

comes down the pier, and she's waving at the crowds and they are loving it all. Then the speeches, mayor first, then the lady, and finally she steps down off the podium and makes for her carriage. Problem. There happens to be a great puddle of slush between her and the brougham, and the red carpet has run out.

You guys should have seen it. The coachman has the door open as wide as the mayor's mouth. McClellan and the opera man Oscar Hammerstein are each side of the French singer and they don't know what to do.

At this point something odd happens. I feel a nudge and a jostle from behind me and someone lays something over my arm, which is resting on the barrier. Whoever he was, he was gone in a second. I never saw him. But what is hanging over my arm is an old opera cape, fusty and tattered, not the sort of thing you'd be carrying or wearing at that hour of the morning, if at all. Then I remembered that as a boy I was given a book called *Heroes Down the Ages*—with pictures. And there was one of a fellow called Raleigh—I guess they named him after the capital of North Carolina. Anyway he once took off his cape and threw it over a puddle right in front of Queen Elizabeth of England and after that he never looked back.

So I think, "If it's good enough for Raleigh it's okay for Mrs. Bloom's little boy," so I leap over the railing round the press area and put the cape right down on the slush in front of this vicomtesse person. Well, she loved it. She walked right over it and got into the cab.

I picked up the wet cape and saw her smiling at me right through the open window. So I thought, "Nothing ventured . . ." and walked up to the window.

"My Lady," says I. That's how you have to talk to these people. "Everyone tells me it is quite impossible to get a personal interview with you. Is that really true?"

That's what you need in this game, guys: flair, charm . . . oh, and looks, of course. What do you mean, I'm okay in a Jewish sort of way? I'm irresistible. Anyway, this is one very beautiful lady and she looks back at me kind of half smiling and I know Hammerstein is growling in the background. But then she whispers, "Tonight at my suite, seven o'clock," and up goes the window. So there we are, I have New York's first exclusive personal interview lined up.

Did I go? Of course I went. But wait, there's more. The mayor tells me to put the cleaning of the cape onto his personal check at the laundry that does all the Gracie Mansion work, and I go back to the *American* feeling pretty pleased. There I met Bernie Smith, our shipping man, and guess what he tells me? When the French lady was thanking McClellan for his welcome Bernie looked up at the warehouses opposite him, and what did he see? A man standing looking down, all alone, like some kind of avenging angel. Before he can go on, I say to Bernie, "Stop right there. He wore a dark cloak right up to the chin, a wide-brim hat and between the two a sort of mask covering most of his face."

Now Bernie's chin drops right down, and he says, "How the hell did you know that?" Then I know for sure I was not hallucinating back in the Tower. There really is a sort of Phantom in this city who lets nobody see his face. I want to know who he is, what he does and why he is so interested in a French opera singer. One day I am going to break that story wide open. Oh, thanks, Harry. Most welcome, cheers. Now, where was I? Oh, yes, my interview with the diva from the Paris Opera.

Ten before seven, there I am in my best suit walking in on the Waldorf-Astoria like I own the place. Right down Peacock Alley towards the main reception desk with the society ladies of the city drifting up and down to see and be seen. Very grand. The main man at reception looks me up and down like I should have been round the back at the tradesmen's entrance.

"Yes?" he says. "Vicomtesse de Chagny's suite, if you please," says I. "Her ladyship is not receiving," says the uniform. "Tell her Mr. Charles Bloom in a different cape is here," says I. Ten seconds on the phone and he is bowing and scraping and insists on escorting me up personally. It just happens there is a bellboy in the lobby with a big parcel tied with ribbon, same destination. So we all go up to the tenth floor together.

Ever been in the Waldorf-Astoria, guys? Well, it is something different. The door is opened by another French lady, personal maid; nice, pretty, with a gimpy leg. She lets me in, takes the parcel and leads me through to the main salon. I tell you, you could play baseball in it. Enormous. Gilt, plush, tapestries, drapes, like part of a palace. The maid says, "Madame is dressing for dinner. She will be with you presently. Please wait here." And I sit on a chair by the wall.

There is no one else in the room except a boy who nods and smiles and says, *"Bon soir,"* so I smile back and say, "Hi." He gets on with his reading while the maid, whose name seems to be Meg, reads the card on the gift-wrapped present. Then she says, "Oh, it's for you, Pierre," and that's when I recognized the kid. He's Madame's son, I saw him earlier at the pier, coming up behind with a priest. He takes the present, starts to unwrap it and Meg goes off through the open door to the bedroom. I can hear the two of them laughing and giggling in there, and speaking French, so I look around the salon.

Flowers everywhere; bouquets from the mayor, from Hammerstein, the opera management board and a host of well-wishers. The boy strips off the ribbon and the paper to reveal a box. This he opens and pulls out a toy. I have nothing else to do, so I watch. It's an odd toy for a boy of twelve going on thirteen. A baseball mitt I could understand, but a toy monkey?

And a very strange monkey at that. It is sitting on a chair and its arms are in front, the hands holding a pair of cymbals. Then I get it: it's mechanical with a wind-up key in the back. Also, it turns out it's a sort of music box, because the boy winds up the key and the monkey starts to play. The arms move back and forward as if it were beating the cymbals together, while from inside it comes a tinkly tune. No problem recognizing it: "Yankee Doodle Dandy."

Now the kid starts to take an interest, holding it up and staring at it from all angles to try and see how it works. When it winds down, he cranks it up and the music starts again. After a while he begins to explore the back of the animal, lifting away a patch of fabric to reveal a sort of panel. Then he comes over to me, very polite, speaking English. "Do you have a penknife, mon-sewer?" he asks. Of course I do. Pencils have to be kept sharp in our game. So I lend him my knife. But instead of cutting the animal open he uses it like a screwdriver to remove four small screws from the back. Now he is looking straight at the mechanism inside. This seems to me a good way of breaking the toy. But this kid is very bright and just wants to find out how the thing works. Me, I have trouble understanding a can opener.

"Very interesting," he says, showing me what is inside, which looks like a mess of wheels, rods, bells, springs and dials. "You see, the turning of the key tightens a coil spring like that of a watch but much bigger and stronger." "Really," I say, just wishing he would close it back up and play "Yankee Doodle" until Mama is ready. But no.

"The power of the unreleased spring is transmitted by a system of rod gears to a turntable here at the base.

On the table there is a disc with various small studs on its upper surface."

"Well, that's great," says I. "Now why not put it back together again?" But he goes on, forehead furrowed in thought as he works it all out. This kid probably understands motor-car engines. "When the studded disc turns, each stud nudges a presprung vertical rod, which is then released and springs back into place, tapping one of these bells as it does so. The bells all have a different pitch, so in the right sequence they make music. Have you ever seen musical bells, m'sieur?"

"Yes. I have seen musical bells. Two or three guys stand in a line behind a long trestle with different bells on it. They pick up a bell, ring it once and put it down. If they get the sequence right, they can play music."

"It's the same theory," says Pierre.

"Well, that's wonderful," says I. "Now why not put it back together again?" But, no, he wants to explore some more. In a few seconds he has extracted the playing disc and holds it up. About the size of a silver dollar, with small knobs all over the surface. He turns it over. More knobs. "See, it must play two tunes, one for each side of the master disc." By now I am convinced this monkey will never play again.

But he puts the disc back, other way up, pokes around with the blade of the knife to make sure everything is touching that should be touching, and closes it back up. Then he winds it up again, puts it on the table and stands back. The monkey starts to wave its arms and play more music. This time a tune I do not know. But someone does.

There is a kind of scream from the bedroom and suddenly the singer lady is in the doorway, in a lace dressing gown, hair tumbling down her back, looking like a million dollars except for the expression on her face, which is like someone who has just seen a very large and fearsome ghost. She stares at the still-playing monkey, rushes across the room, embraces the boy and holds him against her like he was about to be kidnapped.

"What is it?" she asks in a whisper, evidently badly frightened.

"It's a toy monkey, ma'am," says I, trying to be helpful.

" 'Masquerade,' " she whispers. "Twelve years ago. He must be here."

"There's no one here but me, ma'am, and I did not bring it. The toy came in a box, gift-wrapped. The bellboy brought it up." Meg the maid is nodding furiously to confirm what I say.

"Where does it come from?" asks the lady. So I take the monkey, which has now gone silent again, and look all over it. Nothing. Then I try the wrapping paper. Nothing again. So I look all over the cardboard box and right on the underside there is a slip of paper pasted on. It says: S.C. Toys, C.I. Then the old memory checks in. About a year ago last summer I was walking out with a very pretty girl who waited table at

Lombardi's on Spring Street. One day I took her down
to Coney Island for a whole day. Of the various amusement parks we chose Steeplechase. And I recall a toy-
shop there, full of the strangest mechanical toys of all
kinds. There were soldiers that marched, drummers
that drummed, ballet dancers on round drums who
high kicked—you name it, if it could be done with
clockwork and springs, they had it.

So I explained to the lady that I thought S.C. stood
for Steeplechase and C.I. almost certainly stood for
Coney Island. Then I had to explain what Coney Island was all about. She became very thoughtful.
"These . . . sideshows . . . that is what you call them?
They have to do with optical illusions, tricks, trapdoors, secret passages, things mechanical that seem
to work all by themselves?" I nodded. "That's exactly
what sideshows at Coney Island are all about, ma'am."

Then she gets very agitated. "M'sieur Bloom, I
must go there. I must see this toy shop, this Steeplechase Park." I explain there is a rather large problem.
Coney Island is a summer resort only and this is the
start of December. It is closed, shuttered up; the only
work going on is maintenance, repairs, cleaning,
painting, varnishing. Not open to the public. But by
now she is nearly crying and I hate to see a lady in
distress.

So I call up a pal on the commercial desk at the
American and catch him just before he goes home.
Who owns Steeplechase Park? Fellow called George

Tilyou, along with a sleeping and very secret financial partner. Yes, he's getting pretty elderly and no longer lives on the island but in a big house in the borough of Brooklyn. But he still owns Steeplechase Park and has ever since he opened it nine years ago. Does he have a telephone, by any chance? By any chance, he does. So I get the number and place a call. It takes a while, but it comes through and I am talking with Mr. Tilyou personally. I explain everything to him, hinting of the importance to Mayor McClellan that New York should extend every hospitality to Mme. de Chagny . . . Well, you know, a good old-fashioned spiel. Anyway, he says he'll call back.

We wait. An hour. He calls. Different mood entirely, like he had consulted with someone. Yes, he will organize that the gates be opened for one private party. The toy shop will be staffed and the fun master personally will be in attendance at all times. Not possible for the next morning, but the one after.

Well, that means tomorrow, right? So yours truly is going to escort Mme. de Chagny personally down to Coney Island. In fact I would say I am now her private guide to New York itself. And no, guys, there's no point in you all turning up because no one gets to go in but her, me and her personal party. So for one dirty cape I get scoop after scoop. Didn't I tell you this was the best job in the world?

There was only one problem—my exclusive interview, for which I had gone to the hotel in the first place. Did I get it? I did not. The singer lady was so distressed that she rushed back to her bedroom and declined to come out again. Meg the maid offered me her thanks for arranging the trip to Coney Island but said the prima donna was now too tired to continue. So I had to leave. Disappointing, but no matter. I'll get my exclusive tomorrow. And yes, you can get me another pint of the golden brew.

TEN

THE EXULTATION OF ERIK MUHLHEIM

I saw her. After all these years I saw her again and my heart made as if to burst inside me. I stood atop the warehouse near the dock and looked down and there she was, on the quay. Until I caught the glitter of light on the lens of a telescope and had to slip away.

So I went down to the crowd below and fortunately there was such a chill in the air that no one thought anything of a man with his head swathed in a woolly muffler. Thus I was able to approach the brougham, to see her lovely face just a few yards away and to slip my old cloak into the hands of a fool reporter lusting only for his interview.

She was as beautiful as ever: the tiny waist, the tumbling hair tucked up beneath her Cossack hat, the face and smile to break a block of granite clean in two.

Was I right? Was I right to open all the old wounds again, to force myself to bleed again as in that cellar twelve long years ago? Have I been a fool to bring her here when eight score of months had almost cured the pain?

I loved her then, in those fearful hunted years in Paris, more than life itself. The first, and the last and the only love I shall ever have or know. When she rejected me in that cellar for her young vicomte I almost killed them both. The great rage came over me again, that anger that has always been my only companion, my true friend who has never let me down, that rage against God and all His angels that He could not even give me a human face like others, like Raoul de Chagny. A face to smile and please. Instead He gave me this molten mask of horror, a life sentence of isolation and rejection.

And yet I thought, foolish, stupid wretch, that she could even love me just a little, after what had happened between us in that hour of madness while the avenging mob came down to lynch me.

When I knew my fate, I let them live, and glad that I did. But why have I done this now? Surely it can only bring me more pain and rejection, disgust, contempt and repugnance yet again. It is the letter, of course.

Oh, Madame Giry, what am I to think of you now? You were the only person who ever showed me kindness, the only one who did not spit upon me or run screaming from my face. Why did you wait so long? Am I to thank you that in the final hours you sent me the news to change my life again, or to blame you for keeping it from me these past twelve years? I could be dead and gone, and would never have known. But I am not, and now I know. So I take this crazy risk.

To bring her here, to see her again, to suffer again, to ask again, to plead yet again . . . and be rejected yet again? Most probably, most likely. And yet, and yet . . .

I have it here, memorized already word for word; read and reread in dizzy disbelief until the pages are spoiled with sweat and crumpled by trembling hands. Dated in Paris, late in September, just before you died . . .

My dear Erik,

By the time you receive this letter, if you ever do, I shall be gone from the earth and to another place. I wrestled long and hard before deciding to write these lines and only did so because I felt that you, who have known so much misery, should learn the truth at last; and that I could not easily meet my Maker knowing that to the end I had deceived you.

Whether the news contained herein will bring you joy or yet again give only anguish, I cannot tell. But here is the truth of events that were once very close to you and yet of which you could then and since know nothing. Only I, Christine de

Chagny and her husband, Raoul, are aware of this truth and I must beg you to handle it with gentleness and care . . .

Three years after I found a poor wretch of sixteen chained in a cage at Neuilly I met the second of those young men I later came to call my boys. It was by accident, and a dreadful, tragic accident it was.

It was late at night in the winter of 1885. The opera had finally finished, the girls had gone to their quarters, the great building had closed its doors and I was walking home alone through the darkened streets towards my apartment. It was a shortcut, narrow, cobbled and black. Unknown to me there were other people in that alley. Ahead a serving maid, lately dismissed from a house nearby, was trotting fearfully through the dark towards the brighter boulevard ahead. In a doorway a young man who I later learned to be no more than sixteen was saying farewell to the friends with whom he had spent the evening.

Out of the shadows came a ruffian, a footpad such as haunted the back streets looking for a pedestrian to rob of his wallet. Why he picked the little serving girl I shall never know. She could not have had more than five sous on her person. But I saw the rogue run out of the shadows and throw his arm around her throat to stop her screaming while he went for her purse. I yelled, "Leave her alone, brute. *Au secours!*"

The sound of racing male boots went past me, I caught the glimpse of a uniform, and a young man had thrown himself on the footpad, carrying him to the ground. The *midinette* screamed and ran headlong for the lights of the boulevard. I never saw her again. The footpad tore himself loose from the young officer, got to his feet and began to run. The officer rose and went after him. Then I saw the ruffian turn, draw something from his pocket and point it at his pursuer. There was a bang and a flash as he fired. Then he ran through an arch to disappear in the courtyards behind.

I went over to the fallen man and saw that he was little more than a boy, a brave and gallant child, in the uniform of an officer cadet from the École Militaire. His handsome face was white as marble and he was bleeding profusely from a bullet wound in the lower stomach. I tore strips from my petticoat to staunch the bleeding and screamed until a householder looked out from above and asked what was the matter. I urged him to run to the boulevard and hail a cab urgently, which he did in his nightshirt.

It was too far to the Hôtel Dieu, much closer to the Hôspital St. Lazare, so that was where we went. There was one young doctor on duty but when he saw the nature of the wound and learned the identity of the cadet, scion of a most noble family from Normandy, he sent a porter running for a senior surgeon who lived nearby. There was nothing more I could do for the lad, so I went home.

But I prayed that he would live and in the morning, it being a Sunday and no work for me at the opera, I went back to the hospital. The authorities had already sent for the family from Normandy and, seeing me approach, the senior surgeon on duty must have taken me for the cadet's mother when I asked for him by name. His face was a mask of gravity and he asked me to come to his private office. There he told me the dreadful news.

The patient would live, he said, but the damage caused by the bullet and its removal had been terrible. Major blood vessels in the upper groin and lower stomach had been torn beyond repair. He had had no choice but to suture them. Still I did not understand. Then I realized what he meant, and asked in plain language. He nodded solemnly. "I am devastated," he said. "Such a young life, such a handsome boy, and now, alas, only half a man. I fear he will never be able to have a child of his own."

"You mean," I asked, "that the bullet has emasculated him?" The surgeon shook his head. "Even that might have been a mercy, for then he might have felt no desire for a woman. No, he will feel all the passion, the love, the desire that any young man may feel. But the destruction of those vital blood vessels means that . . ."

"I am no child myself, M'sieur le Docteur," I said, wishing to spare his embarrassment though I knew with awful dread what was coming.

"Then, madame, I must tell you that he will never be able to consummate any union with a woman and thus create a child of his own."

"So he can now never marry?" I asked. The surgeon shrugged.

"It would be a strange and saintly woman, or one with a powerful other motive, who could accept such a union with no physical dimension," he said. "I am truly sorry. I did what I did to save his life from the hemorrhage."

I could hardly keep from weeping at the tragedy of it. That such a foul fiend could inflict so dreadful a wound on a boy at the threshold of life seemed impossible. But I went to see the boy anyway. He was pale and weak, but awake. He had not been told. He thanked me prettily for helping him in the alley, insisting that I had saved his life. When I heard his family arriving hotfoot from the Rouen train I left.

I never thought to see my young aristocrat again but I was wrong. Eight years later, grown handsome as a Greek god, he began to frequent the Opera night after night, hoping for a word and a smile from a certain understudy. Later, finding her with child, good, kind and decent man that he was, he confessed all to her and with her agreement married her, giving her his name, his title and a wedding band. And for twelve years he has given to the son all the love a real father could ever give.

So there you have the truth, my poor Erik. Try to be kind and gentle.

From one who tried to help you in your pain,
A dying kiss,
Antoinette Giry

I will see her tomorrow. She must know it by now. The message to the hotel was plain enough. She would know that musical monkey anywhere. The place of my choosing, of course; the hour of my selection. Will she be frightened of me still? I suppose so. Yet she will not know how fearful I will be of her; of her power to deny me again some tiny measure of the happiness most men can take for granted.

But even if I am to be repulsed yet again, everything has changed. I can look down from this high eyrie onto the heads of that human race I so loathe, but now I can say: You can spit on me, defile me; jeer at me, revile me; but nothing you can do will hurt me now. Through the filth and through the rain, through the tears and through the pain, my life's not been in vain; *I have a son.*

ELEVEN

THE
PRIVATE DIARY OF
MEG GIRY

Dear Diary,

At last I am able to sit down in peace and confide to you my inner thoughts and worries, for it is now the small hours of the morning and everyone is abed.

Pierre is fast asleep, quiet as a lamb, for I peeped in ten minutes ago. Father Joe I can hear snoring away in his cot next to where I am sitting and even the thick walls of this hotel do not deny his farm-boy snorts. And Madame is at last asleep also with a cachet to help her find rest. For in twelve years I have never seen her so distressed.

It all had to do with that toy monkey that some

anonymous donor sent to Pierre here in the suite. There was a reporter here also, very nice and helpful (and who flirted with his eyes at me), but that was not what upset Madame so badly. It was the toy monkey.

When she had heard it play its second tune—the sounds of which came straight through the open door into the boudoir where I was brushing her hair—she became like one possessed. She insisted on finding out from where it came, and when the reporter, M. Bloom, had traced it and arranged a visit, she insisted that she be left alone. I had to ask the young man to leave, and get Pierre protesting into bed.

After that, I found her at her dressing table, staring at the mirror but making no attempt to complete her toilette. So I canceled dinner in the restaurant with Mr. Hammerstein also.

Only when we were alone could I ask her what was going on. For this journey to New York, which started so well and saw such a fine reception at the quay earlier in the day, had turned to something dark and sinister.

Of course, I too recognized the strange monkey doll and the haunting tune it played, and it brought back a tidal wave of frightening memories. Thirteen years . . . that was what she kept repeating as we talked, and truly it has been thirteen years since those strange events that culminated in the terrible descent to the lowest and darkest cellar beneath the Paris Opera. But though I was there that night, and have tried to question Madame since, she has always kept her silence and

I never did learn the details of the relationship between her and the frightening figure we chorus girls used to refer to simply as the Phantom.

Until this night when at last she told me more. Thirteen years ago she was involved in a truly remarkable scandal at the Paris Opera when she was abducted right from the center of the stage during the performance of a new opera, *Don Juan Triumphant*, which has never been repeated since.

I was myself in the corps de ballet that night, though I was not onstage at the moment the lights fused out and she disappeared. Her abductor carried her from the stage down to the deepest cellars of the Opera, where she was later rescued by the gendarmes and the rest of the cast, headed by the *commissaire de police* who happened to be in the audience.

I was there too, trembling with fear as we all came down with burning torches, through cellar after cellar until we reached the lowest catacomb by the underground lake. We expected to find at last the dreaded Phantom but all we and the gendarmes found was Madame, alone and shaking like a leaf, and later Raoul de Chagny who had come ahead of us and seen the Phantom face-to-face.

There was a chair, with a cloak thrown over it, and we thought the monster might be hiding underneath. But no. Just a monkey toy, with cymbals and a musical box inside. The police took it away as evidence and I never saw such a one again, until this night.

That was the time she was being daily courted by

the young Vicomte Raoul de Chagny and all the girls were so envious of her. Had it not been for her beautiful nature she might well have invited hostility too, for her looks, her sudden leap to stardom and the love of the most eligible bachelor in Paris. But no one hated her; we all loved her and were delighted to see her restored to us. But though we became closer over the years, she never mentioned what happened to her in the hours that she was missing, and her only explanation was that "Raoul rescued me." So what was the significance of the toy monkey?

This night I knew better than to ask her directly, so I fussed about and brought her a little food, which she refused to eat. When I had persuaded her to take her sleeping draught she became drowsy and let slip for the first time a few details of those bizarre events.

She told me there had been another man, a strange elusive creature who frightened, fascinated, overawed and helped her, but who had an obsessional love for her that she could not repay. Even as a chorus girl I had heard tales of a strange phantom who haunted the lower cellars of the Opera and had amazing powers, being able to come and go unseen and inflict his will on the management by threats of retribution if they did not obey him. The man and his legend frightened us all, but I never knew he loved my mistress of today in such a manner. I asked about the monkey that played a haunting tune.

She said she had only seen such a creature once before, and I am sure that it must have been during those hours in the cellars with the monster, the same one I myself found on the empty chair.

As the sleep came over her, she kept repeating that "he" must be back: alive and close, moving behind the scenes as ever, a terrifying genius of a man, as fearsomely ugly as her Raoul was handsome, the one she had rejected and who had now lured her to New York to confront her again.

I will do everything I can to protect her, for she is my friend as well as my employer and she is good and kind. But now I am frightened, for there is something or someone out there in the night and I fear for all of us: for me, for Father Joe, for Pierre and most of all her, Madame.

The last thing she said to me before she slipped away into sleep was that for the sake of Pierre and of Raoul she must find the strength to refuse him again, for she is convinced that soon he will at last appear and demand her again. I pray that she has that strength and I pray that these next ten days will hurry past so that we may all return safely to the security of Paris and away from this place of monkeys that play long-ago tunes and the unseen presence of the Phantom.

TWELVE

THE JOURNAL OF TAFFY JONES

STEEPLECHASE PARK, CONEY ISLAND,
DECEMBER 1, 1906

Mine is a strange job and some would say not for a man of some intelligence and no small ambition. For this reason I have often been tempted to give it up and move on to something else. Yet I have never done so in the nine years since I have been employed here at Steeplechase Park.

Part of this reason is that the job offers security for me and my wife and brood, with an excellent income and comfortable living conditions. Another part is that I have simply come to enjoy it. I enjoy the laughter of the children and the pleasure of their parents. I take satisfaction in the simple off-duty happiness of those

all around me during the summer months and the con-
trasting peace and quiet of the winter season.

As for my living conditions, they could hardly be
more comfortable for a man of my station. My principal dwelling is a snug cottage in the respectable
middle-class community of Brighton Beach, barely a
mile from my place of work. Add to that, I have a
small cabin here in the heart of the fair to which I can
repair for a rest from time to time, even at the height
of the season. As for my salary, it is generous. Ever
since, three years ago, I negotiated a reward based on
a tiny fraction of the gate money, I have been able to
take home over one hundred dollars a week.

Being a man of modest tastes and not much of a
drinker, I am able to put a good part of it by, so that
one day and not so many years from now I shall be
able to retire from all this, with my five children off
my hands and making their way in the world. Then I
shall take my Blodwyn and we will find a small farm,
perhaps by a river or a lake or even by the sea, where
I can farm and fish as the mood takes me, and go to
chapel on the Sabbath and be a regular pillar of the
local society. And so I stay and do my job, which most
say I do very well.

For I am the official fun master of Steeplechase Park.
Which means that with my extra long shoes on my
feet, my baggy trousers in a violent check, my stars-
and-stripes weskit and my tall top hat I stand at the
entrance gate to the park and welcome all visitors.

More, with my bushy sideburns and handlebar mustache and a smile of cheerful welcome on my face, I bring many of them in who would otherwise have passed by.

Using my megaphone I cry constantly, "Roll up, roll up, all the fun of the fair, thrills and spills, strange and wonderful things to see, come in my friends and have the time of your lives . . ." and so on and on. Up and down outside the gate I go, greeting and welcoming the pretty girls in their best summer frocks and the young men trying so hard to impress them in striped jackets and straw boaters; and the families with their children clamoring for the many and special treats that I tell them are in store once they have persuaded their parents to take them in. And in they go, paying their nickels and dimes at the pay booths, and of every fifty cents there is one for me.

Of course, this is a summer job, lasting from April until October, when the first cold winds come in off the Atlantic and we close down for the winter.

Then I can hang the fun master's suit in the closet and drop the Welsh lilt that the visitors find so charming, for I was born in Brooklyn and have never seen the land of my father and his fathers before him. Then I can come to work in a normal suit and supervise the winter program when all the sideshows and rides are dismantled and stored; when the machinery is serviced and greased, worn parts replaced, timber sanded and repainted or varnished, carousel horses regilded and torn canvas stitched. By the time April comes again all is back where it should be and the gates open with the first warm and sunny days.

So it was with some amazement that two days ago I received a letter from Mr. George Tilyou personally, he being the gentleman who owns the park. He dreamed up the idea in the first place, with a partner who exists only in rumor and whom the world has never seen, at least not down here. It was Mr. T.'s energy and vision that brought it all into being nine years ago and since then the park has made him a very rich man indeed.

His letter came by personal delivery and was clearly very urgent. It explained that on the following day, which of course is now yesterday, a private party would be visiting the park and for these people the place should be opened up. He said he knew the rides and carousels could not function in time, but stressed that the toy shop should be open and fully staffed and so also should the Hall of Mirrors. And this letter led to the strangest day I have ever known in Steeplechase Park.

Mr. Tilyou's instructions that the toy shop and the Hall of Mirrors should be fully staffed put me in the very devil of a fix. For both my key staff in these areas are on vacation and far away.

Nor are they easily replaceable. The mechanical toys in the shop, the very speciality of that emporium, are not only the most sophisticated in all America but are also very complicated. It takes a real expert to understand them and explain their workings to the young people who come by to wonder, to explore and to buy. I am certainly not that expert. I could only hope for the best—or so I thought.

Of course the place is bitter cold in winter but I took kerosene warmers in to heat the shop up on the evening before the visit so that by dawn it was warm as a summer's day. Then I removed all the dust sheets from the shelves to reveal the ranks of clockwork soldiers, drummers, dancers, acrobats and animals that sing, dance and play. But that was as far as I could go. I had done all I could in the toy shop by eight in the morning before the private party were due to arrive. Then something most strange happened.

I turned around to find a young man staring at me. I do not know how he had got in, and was about to tell him that the place was closed when he offered to operate the toy shop for me. How did he know I had visitors coming? He did not say. He just explained that he had worked here once and understood the mechanics of all the toys. Well, with the regular toy man missing, I had no choice but to accept. He did not look like the toy man, all jovial and welcoming and a favorite with the kids. He had a bone-white face, black hair and eyes and a black formal coat. I asked for his name. He paused for a second and said, "Malta." So that is what I called him until he left, or rather vanished. But more later.

The Hall of Mirrors was another matter. It is a most amazing place and though, in off-duty hours, I have been inside it myself I have never been able to understand how it works. Whoever designed it must have been a sort of genius. All visitors have come out after a ritual stroll through the many constantly changing mirror rooms convinced they have seen things they could not have seen and not seen things that must have been there. It is a house not just of mirrors but of illusion. In case, years from now, any soul should read this journal, having some interest in the Coney Island that once was, let me try to explain the Hall of Mirrors.

From the outside it appears a simple, low-built square building with one door for going in and out. Once inside, the visitor sees a corridor running to his left and right. It matters not which way he turns. Both walls of the corridor are sheeted with mirror and the passage is exactly four feet wide. This is important, for the inner wall is not unbroken but composed of vertical sheets of mirror exactly eight feet wide and seven high. Each plate is on a vertical axis, so that when one is turned by remote control half of it will completely block the passage, but reveal a new passage heading into the heart of the building.

He has no choice but to follow this new passage which, as the plates turn on a secret command, become more and more passages, small rooms of mirrors that appear and disappear. But it gets worse. For nearer the center many of the eight-feet-wide sheets are not only axled top to bottom but stand on eight-feet-diameter discs which themselves revolve. A visitor, standing on a semicircular but unseen disc with his back to a mirror, may find himself turned through ninety, a hundred eighty, or two hundred seventy degrees. He thinks he is stationary and only the mirrors are turning, but to him other people suddenly appear and disappear; small rooms are created, then dissolve; he addresses a stranger who appears before him only to realize he is talking to the image of someone behind him or to his side.

Husbands and wives, lovers and sweethearts are separated in seconds, stumble forward to be reunited—but with someone quite different. Screams of fright and laughter echo throughout the hall when a dozen young couples have ventured in together.

Now all this is controlled by the mirror man, who alone understands how it all works. He sits in a raised booth above the door and by glancing upwards can see a roof mirror, angled to give him alone a bird's-eye view of the whole floor, so that with a bank of levers under his hand he can create and dissolve the passages, rooms and illusions. My problem was that Mr. Tilyou had insisted the lady visitor should under all circumstances be urged to visit the Hall of Mirrors, but the mirror man was on holiday and could not be contacted.

I had to try to understand the controls myself so that I could operate them for the lady's amusement, and to this end spent half the night inside the building with a paraffin lantern, testing and experimenting with the levers until I was sure I could guide the lady for a quick tour inside and yet show her the way out when she cried for release. For with the rooms of mirrors all open-topped, the sound of voices is quite clear.

By nine yesterday morning I had done the best I could and was waiting to greet Mr. Tilyou's personal guests. They came just before the hour of ten. There was virtually no traffic on Surf Avenue and when I saw the brougham coming past the offices of *Brooklyn Eagle*, past the entrances to Luna Park and Dreamland and on towards me down the avenue, I presumed it must be they. For the brougham was the smartly painted hack that waits outside the Manhattan Beach Hotel for those descending from the El train from the Brooklyn Bridge, though few enough there are in December.

As it approached and the driver reined in his pair I stepped forward with the megaphone up. "Welcome, welcome, ladies and gentlemen, to Steeplechase Park, first and finest of the amusement parks on Coney Island," I boomed, though even the horses gave me a glance as if looking at a madman dressed in all his finery at the end of November.

The first out of the coach was a young man who turned out to be a reporter from the *New York American,* one of Hearst's yellow-press rags. Very full of himself he was and apparently the visitors' guide to New York. Next out came a most beautiful lady, a true aristocrat—oh, yes, you can always tell—whom the reporter presented as the Vicomtesse de Chagny and one of the leading opera singers in the world. Of course I did not need to be told this, for I read *The New York Times*, being myself a man of some education, even though self-taught. Only then did I understand why Mr. Tilyou wished to indulge the wishes of such a lady. She descended to the rain-slick boardwalk, supported on the arm of the reporter; I laid down the megaphone—no further use for it—gave her a most sweeping bow and welcomed her again to my domain. She replied with a smile to melt the stone heart of Cader Idris and said in a delightful French accent that she regretted having to disturb my winter hibernation. "Your devoted servant, ma'am," I replied to show that behind my fun-master clothes I was aware of proper forms of address.

Next came a small boy of about twelve or thirteen, a good-looking lad who was also French like his mother but spoke excellent English. He was clutching a toy monkey cum music box of the type I saw at once must have come from our own toy shop, the only place in all New York to provide them. For a moment I was worried: had it broken down? Were they here to complain?

The reason for the boy's good English emerged last, a stocky and fit-looking Irish priest in black cassock and broad hat. "A good morning to you, Mr. Fun Master," said he. "And a cold one for the likes of us to bring you out."

"But not cold enough to chill a warm Irish heart," said I, not to be outdone, for as a chapel going man I do not normally have much to do with Papist priests. But he threw back his head and roared with laughter, so I reckoned he was perhaps a good fellow after all.

It was thus in a merry mood that I led the party of four up the boardwalk, through the gates, past the open turnstile and towards the toy shop, for it was plain this was what they wished to see.

Thanks to the heaters it was pleasantly warm inside and Mr. Malta was waiting to greet them. At once the boy, whose name turned out to be Pierre, was entranced by the shelves and shelves of mechanical dancers, soldiers, musicians, clowns and animals that are the glory of the Steeplechase toy shop and not to be found anywhere else in the city and perhaps not in all the country. He was racing up and down the alleys asking to be shown them all. But his mother was only interested in one type—the rack of music-playing monkeys.

We found them on a rear shelf, right at the back, and she at once asked Mr. Malta to make them play.

"All of them?" he asked.

"One after the other," she said firmly. So it was done. One after the other the keys in the backs were wound up and the monkeys began to bang their cymbals and play their tune. "Yankee Doodle Dandy," always the same. I was puzzled. Did she want a substitute? And did not they all sound the same? Then she nodded at her son and he produced a penknife with a screwdriver attachment. Malta and I looked on stunned as the boy eased away a flap of cloth at the back of the first monkey, then undid a small panel and put his hand inside. He took out a silver-dollar-sized disc, flipped it over and put it back. I raised my eyebrows to Malta and he did the same. The monkey began to play again. "Song of Dixie." Of course, one tune for the North and one for the South.

He soon replaced the disc the way it had been, and started on the second. Same result. After ten his mother signaled at him to stop. Malta began to replace the wares as they had been before. Clearly not even he knew there were two tunes inside the monkey. The vicomtesse was very pale. "He has been here," she said to no one in particular. Then to me, "Who designed and made these monkeys?"

I shrugged in ignorance. Then Malta said, "They are made by a small factory in New Jersey, all of them. But under license and from patented designs. As for who designed them, I do not know."

Then the lady asked, "Have either of you ever seen a strange man here? A man in a wide hat, with most of his face covered by a mask?"

At this last question I felt Mr. Malta, who was standing beside me, stiffen like a ramrod. I glanced at him but his face was as set as stone. So I shook my head and explained to her that in a fair there are many masks: clown masks, monster masks, Hallowe'en masks. But a man who wore a mask all the time, just to cover his face? No, never. At this point she sighed and shrugged, then wandered off down the aisles between the shelves to look at the other toys.

Malta beckoned to the boy and led him away in the other direction, apparently to show him a display of clockwork marching soldiers. But I was beginning to have my doubts about this icy young man so I slipped after them while keeping a rack of toys between us. To my surprise and annoyance my unexpected and mysterious helper began quietly to interrogate the child, who answered innocently enough.

"Just why has your mama come to New York?" he asked.

"Why, to sing in the opera, sir."

"Indeed. And no other reason? Not to meet anyone special?"

"No, sir."

"And why is she interested in monkeys that play tunes?"

"Only one monkey, monsieur, and one tune. But that is the one she is holding now. No other monkey plays the tune she seeks."

"How sad. And your papa, is he not here?"

"No, sir. Dear Papa was detained in France. He arrives by sea tomorrow."

"Excellent. And he really is your papa?"

"Of course. He is married to Mama and I am his son."

At this point I felt the impudence had gone far enough and was about to intervene when something strange happened. The door came open, admitting a blast of cold air off the sea, and in the frame was the stocky figure of the priest, who I had learned was called Father Kilfoyle. Feeling the chill air, the boy Pierre and Mr. Malta came into sight from around the corner of one of the display racks. The priest and the white-faced one were ten yards apart and stared at each other. At once the priest raised his right hand and made the sign of the cross over his forehead and chest. As a good chapel man, I do not go along with all this, but I know that for Catholics it is a sign of seeking the Lord's protection.

Then the priest said, "Come, now, Pierre," and held out his hand. But he was still staring at Mr. Malta.

The clear confrontation between the two men, which was to be the first of two that day, had cast as good a chill as the wind off the sea, so in an attempt to restore the mood of merriment of just an hour before, I said: "Your ladyship, our pride and joy here is the Hall of Mirrors, a true wonder of the world. Please allow me to show it to you, it will restore your spirits. And Master Pierre can amuse himself with the other toys, for as you see he is quite enchanted as are all young people who come in here."

She seemed undecided and I recalled with some trepidation how insistent Mr. Tilyou had been in his letter that she should see the mirrors, though I could not discern why. She glanced at the Irishman, who nodded, and said, "Sure, see the wonder of the world for a while. I'll look after Pierre, and we have the time. Rehearsals are not till after lunch." So she nodded and came with me.

If the episode in the toy shop was strange, the boy and his mother seeking a tune that none of the monkeys could play, what followed was truly bizarre and explains why I have been at pains to describe exactly what I saw and heard that day.

We entered the hall together through the only door and she saw the corridor left and right. I gestured that she should make her choice. She shrugged, smiled most prettily and turned to the right. I climbed to the control box and glanced into the upper mirror. I could see she had reached a point halfway down one of the side walls. I moved a lever to turn a mirror and direct her towards the center. Nothing happened. I tried again. Still nothing. The controls did not work. I could see her still moving between the mirror walls of the outer passage. Then a mirror swung of its own accord, blocking her path and forcing her towards the center. But I had moved nothing. Clearly the controls were malfunctioning and for her own safety it was time to let her out before she became trapped. I moved the levers to create a straight passage back to the door. Nothing happened, but inside the maze mirrors *were* moving, as if under their own control or that of someone else. I could see twenty images of the young woman as more and more mirrors spun, but now I could not work out which was the real person and which the image.

Suddenly she stopped, trapped in a small center room. There was another movement in one wall of that room and I caught a swirl of a cloak, replicated twenty times, just before it vanished again. But it was not her cloak, for it was black while hers was of plum velvet. I saw her eyes open wide and her hand flew to her mouth. She was staring at something or someone standing with his back to a mirror plate, but in the one blind spot that my observation glass could not cover. Then she spoke. "Oh, it *is* you," she said. I realized that somehow another person had not only entered the hall but found a way to the center of the maze without being observed by me. This was impossible, until I saw that the angle of the tilted mirror above and ahead of me had been altered in the night so that it covered only one half of the hall. The other half was out of vision. I could see her, but not the phantom to whom she spoke. And I could hear them, so I have tried to recall and note down exactly what was said.

There was something else. This woman from France, rich, famous, talented and poised, was actually trembling. I sensed her fear but it was fear mixed with a dreadful fascination. As the later overheard conversation showed, she had met someone from her past, someone she had thought to be free from, someone who had once held her in a web . . . of what? Fear, yes, that I could feel in the air. Love? Perhaps, once, long ago. And awe. Whoever he was, whoever he had once been, she still stood in awe of his power and personality. Several times I could see her shivering and yet he offered her no threat that I could hear. But this is what they said:

HE: Of course. Did you suspect another?
SHE: After the monkey, no. To hear "Masquerade" again . . . It has been so long.
HE: Thirteen long years. Have you thought of me?

SHE: Of course, my Master of Music. But I thought . . .

HE: That I was dead? No, Christine, my love, not me.

SHE: My love? Do you still? . . .

HE: Always and for ever, until I die. In spirit you are still mine, Christine. I made the singing star but could not keep her.

SHE: When you vanished I thought you had gone forever. I married Raoul? . . .

HE: I know. I have followed every step, every move, every triumph.

SHE: Has it been hard for you, Erik?

HE: Hard enough. My road has always been harder than you will ever know.

SHE: You brought me here? The Opera, it is yours?

HE: Yes. All mine, and more, much more. Wealth to buy half of France.

SHE: Why, Erik, oh, why did you do it? Could you not leave me be? What do you want of me?

HE: Stay with me.

SHE: I cannot.

HE: Stay with me, Christine. Times have changed. I can offer you every opera house in the world. Everything you could ever ask for.

SHE: I cannot. I love Raoul. Try to accept that. All you have ever done for me I remember and with gratitude. But my heart lies elsewhere and always will. Cannot you understand that? Can you not accept?

At this point there was a long pause as if the suitor who had been turned down was trying to recover from his grief. When he resumed there was a tremor in the voice.

HE: Very well. Accept I must. Why not, my heart has been broken so many times. But there is one more thing. Leave me my boy.

SHE: Your . . . boy? . . .

HE: My son, our son, Pierre.

The woman, whom I could still see, indeed reflected a dozen times, went white as a sheet and threw both her hands up to cover her face. She rocked for several seconds and I feared she would faint. I was about to cry out, but my call died in my throat. I was a mute and helpless witness of something I could not understand. Finally she removed her hands and spoke in a whisper.

SHE: Who told you?

HE: Madame Giry.

SHE: Why, oh, why did she do it?

HE: She was dying. She wanted to share the secret of so many years.

SHE: She lied.

HE: No. She tended Raoul after the shooting in the alley.

SHE: He is a good, kind and gentle man. He has loved me and brought up Pierre as his own. Pierre does not know.

HE: Raoul knows. You know. I know. Leave me my son.

SHE: I cannot, Erik. He will soon be thirteen. In five years more, a man. Then I will tell him. You have my word, Erik. On his eighteenth birthday. Not yet, he is not ready. He needs me still. When he is told, he will choose.

HE: I have your word, Christine? If I wait five years . . .

SHE: You will have your son. In five years. If you can win him.

HE: Then I will wait. I have waited so long for one tiny fragment of the happiness most men can learn at their father's knee. Five years more . . . I will wait.

SHE: Thank you, Erik. In three days I will sing for you again. You will be there?

HE: Of course. Closer than you can know.

SHE: Then I will sing for you as I have never sung before.

Now at this point I saw something that almost caused me to fall out of my control booth. Somehow a second man had managed to creep into the hall. How he did it I will never know, but it was not through the only door known to me for that was right below me and had not been used. He must have slipped in by that secret entrance that only the designer of the place could ever know existed and which had never been revealed to anyone else. I thought at first I might be seeing a reflection of the speaker, but I recalled a swirl of cloak or cape, and this figure, also in black, wore no cape but a tight black frock coat. He was in one of the inner passages and I saw that he was crouched with his ear to the hairline crack separating two mirrors beside him. Beyond the crack was the inner mirror room where the lady and her strange former lover had been talking.

He seemed to feel my eyes upon him, for he turned suddenly, stared all around and then glanced up. The tilted observation mirror revealed him to me and me to him. The hair was as black as his coat and his face as white as his shirt. It was the wretch who called himself Malta. Two blazing eyes fixed me for a second, then he was off, speeding through the corridors that others found so baffling. I came down from the booth at once in an attempt to stop him, let myself out and hastened round the building. He was well ahead of me, having escaped through his secret exit, and haring for the gate. In my great clumsy extralong fun master's boots, running was out of the question.

So I could only watch. There was a second carriage parked near the gate, a closed calash, and it was to this that the speeding figure ran, jumping inside, then slamming the door as the carriage took off. It was evidently a private rig for such are not for public hire on Coney Island.

But before he reached it, he had to run past two people. The nearest to the Hall of Mirrors was the young reporter and as the figure in the frock coat raced past he let out a sort of shout which I could not catch, the sound being borne away on the sea wind. The reporter looked up in surprise but made no move to stop the man.

Just before the gateway was the figure of the priest, who had taken the boy Pierre back to the coach, closed him inside and was walking back to find his employer. I saw the fugitive stop dead for a second and stare at the priest, who stared back at him, then run on towards his rig.

By now my nerves were in a complete jangle. The odd search among the performing monkeys for a tune that none of them was able to play, the even odder behavior of the man who called himself Malta in his interrogation of the harmless child, the hate-filled confrontation between Malta and the Catholic priest, and then the catastrophe of the Hall of Mirrors, with all the levers out of my control, the terrible confessions I had heard from the prima donna and a man who had clearly once been her lover and the father of her child, and finally the sight of Malta eavesdropping on them both . . . it was all too much. In my perplexity I completely forgot that poor Mme. de Chagny was still trapped inside the maze of mirrored walls.

When I remembered this, I rushed back to liberate her. All the controls were miraculously working again and soon she emerged, deathly pale and quiet, as well she might be. But she thanked me most politely for all my trouble, left a generous gratuity and boarded her brougham with the reporter, the priest and her son. I escorted her as far as the gate.

When I returned to the Hall of Mirrors for the last time I received the shock of my life. Standing in the lee of the building, staring after the carriage that bore away his son, was the man. I came round the corner of the building and there he was. No doubt about it; the swirling black cloak gave him away. The other player in the weird events that had taken place inside the maze. But it was his face that set my blood running cold. A ravaged face, three-quarters covered by a pale mask and behind the mask burned eyes that blazed with anger. This was a man who had been thwarted, a man not accustomed to being crossed and who had become dangerous. He did not seem to hear me for he muttered something in a low growl. "Five years," I heard him say, "five years. Never. He's mine and I will have him with me."

He turned and was gone, twisting between two stalls and a shuttered roundabout. Later I found a point in the fence onto Surf Avenue where three palisades had been removed. I never saw him after that, and I never saw the eavesdropper again.

I deliberated later if there was anything I should do. Should I alert the vicomtesse that the strange man seemed to have no intention of waiting five years for his son? Or would he calm down when his anger cooled? Whatever I had heard was a family matter and would no doubt be resolved. So I sought to tell myself.

But there is not Celtic blood in my veins for nothing, and even as I write all those things that I saw and heard here yesterday, there hangs over me a sense of terrible foreboding.

THIRTEEN

THE ECSTASY AND PRAYER OF JOSEPH KILFOYLE

"Lord have mercy, Christ have mercy. Many times I have called upon You. More times than I can recall. In the heat of the sun and in the darkness of the night. In the high mass in Your house and in the privacy of my room. Sometimes I even thought You might reply, seemed to hear Your voice, seemed to feel Your guidance. Was it all foolishness, self-delusion? Do we really, in prayer, commune with You? Or are we listening to ourselves?

"Forgive my doubting, Lord. I try so hard for true faith. Hear me now, I beg You. For I am bewildered and frightened. It is not the scholar but the Irish farm boy that I was born. Please listen and help me."

"I am here, Joseph. What disturbs your peace of mind?"

"Lord, for the first time I think I am really frightened. I am afraid but I do not know why."

"Fear? That is something of which I have personal knowledge."

"You, Lord? Surely not."

"On the contrary. What do you think I felt when they tied my wrists above me to the flogging ring in the temple wall?"

"I just did not imagine that You could feel fear."

"I was a man then, Joseph. With all a man's weaknesses and flaws. That was the whole point. And a man can feel great fear. So when they showed me the scourge, with its knotted thongs set with fragments of iron and lead, and told me what it would do, I cried from fear."

"I never thought of it that way, Lord. It was never reported."

"A small mercy. Why are you afraid?"

"I feel there is something going on around me in this fearsome city that I cannot understand."

"Then I sympathize. The fear of what you can understand is bad enough, but it has its limits. The other fear is worse. What do you want of me?"

"I need Your fortitude, Your strength."

"You already have them, Joseph. You inherited them when you took my vows and wore my cloth."

"Then surely I cannot be worthy of them, Lord, for

they escape me now. I fear You chose a poor vessel when You picked the farm boy from Mullingar."

"In fact, you chose me. But no matter. Has my vessel cracked and let me down so far?"

"I have sinned, of course."

"Of course. Who does not? You have lusted after Christine de Chagny."

"She is a beautiful woman, Lord, and I am also a man."

"I know. I was, once. It can be very hard. You confessed and were forgiven?"

"Yes."

"Well, thoughts are thoughts. You did nothing more?"

"No, Lord. Just thoughts."

"Well, then, perhaps I may retain confidence in my farm boy a mite longer. What of your unexplained fears?"

"There is a man in this city, a strange man. The day we arrived I looked up from the quayside and saw a figure on the roof of a warehouse, staring down. He wore a mask. Yesterday we went to Coney Island; Christine, young Pierre, a local reporter and myself. Christine went into a part of the fair known as the Hall of Mirrors. Last night she asked for confession and told me . . ."

"I think you are allowed to tell me, as I am inside your own head. Go on."

"That she had met him inside. She described him.

He must have been the same man, the one she knew years ago in Paris, a badly disfigured man, now become rich and powerful here in New York."

"I know him. His name is Erik. He has not had an easy life. Now he worships another god."

"There are no other gods, Lord."

"Nice idea, but there are many. Man-made gods."

"Ah. And his?"

"He is the servant of Mammon, the god of greed and gold."

"I would dearly love to bring him back. To you."

"Most commendable. And why?"

"It seems he has enormous wealth, riches beyond normal dreams."

"Joseph, you are supposed to be in the business of souls, not gold. Do you lust after his fortune?"

"Not for myself, Lord. For something else."

"And what might that be?"

"While I have been here I wandered by night through the Lower East Side district of this city, but a few miles from this very cathedral. It is an appalling place, an inferno on earth. There is grinding poverty, squalor, filth, stench and despair. Out of these come every vice and crime. Children are used as prostitutes, boys and girls . . ."

"Do I hear a hint of rebuke, Joseph, that I should allow these things?"

"I could not rebuke You, Lord."

"Oh, don't be too modest. It happens every day."

"But I cannot understand it."

"Let me try to explain. I never gave Man a guarantee of perfection, only the chance of it. That was the whole point of it all. Man has the choice and the chance but never the coercion. I have left his freedom to choose inviolate. Some choose to try to follow the path I pointed out; most prefer their pleasures now, here. For many that means inflicting pain on others for their own amusement or enrichment. It is noted, of course, but is not to be changed."

"But why, Lord, can Man not be a better creature?"

"Look, Joseph, if I reached down and touched him on the forehead and made him perfect, what would life on earth be like? No sadness, so no joy. No tears, no smiles. No pain, no relief. No bondage, no freedom. No failure, no triumph. No rudeness, no courtesy. No bigotry, no tolerance. No despair, no exultation. No sin and certainly no redemption. I would simply create a paradise of featureless bliss here on earth, which would make my heavenly kingdom somewhat redundant. And that is not the point of it all. So, Man must have his choice, until I call him home."

"I suppose so, Lord. But I would dearly like to bring this Erik and all his riches to a better service."

"Perhaps you will."

"But there must be a key."

"Of course, there is always a key."

"But I cannot see it, Lord."

"You have read my words. Have you taken nothing in?"

"Too little, Lord. Help me. Please."

"The key is love, Joseph. The key is always love."

"But he loves Christine de Chagny."

"So?"

"Am I to encourage her to break her marriage vows?"

"I did not say that."

"Then I do not understand."

"You will, Joseph, you will. Sometimes it takes a little patience. So, this Erik frightens you?"

"No, Lord, not he. When I saw him on the roof and later saw his figure fleeing from the Hall of Mirrors, I felt there was something about him: a feeling of rage, of despair, of pain. But not of evil. It was the other one."

"Tell me about the other one."

"When we arrived at the Coney Island funfair, Christine and Pierre went into the toy shop with the fun master. I stayed outside to walk by the sea for a while. When I rejoined them in the shop, Pierre was with a young man who was showing him round and whispering in his ear. A face as white as bone, black eyes and hair, a black frock coat. I thought he was the manager of the shop, but the fun master told me later he had never seen him before that morning."

"And you did not like him, Joseph?"

"Liking was not the point, Lord. There was something about him, a chill colder than the sea. Was it just my Hibernian imagination? There was an aura of evil about him that caused me to make Your sign, just instinctively. I took the boy away from him and he stared at me with a dark loathing. That was the first time I saw him that day."

"And the second?"

"I was walking back from the coach where I had put the boy. About half an hour later. I knew Christine had gone with the fun master to examine a sideshow called the Hall of Mirrors. A small door in the side of the building opened, and he came running out. He went past a newspaper reporter who was ahead of me and as he came past me to throw himself into a small coach and disappear, he stopped and stared at me again. It was the same as the first time; I felt the day, already cold, had dropped another ten degrees. I shivered. Who was he? What does he want?"

"I think you mean Darius. Do you wish to redeem him too?"

"I do not think I could."

"You are right. He has sold his soul to Mammon, he is the god of gold's eternal servant, until he comes to me. It was he who brought Erik to his own god. But Darius has no love. That is the difference."

"But he loves gold, Lord."

"No, he worships gold. There is a difference. Erik worships gold also, but somewhere deep inside his tortured soul he once knew love, and could again."

"Then I might yet win him?"

"Joseph, no man who can know pure love, excepting only love of self, is beyond redemption."

"But like Darius, this Erik loves only gold, himself and another's wife. Lord, I do not understand."

FREDERICK FORSYTH

"You are wrong, Joseph. He cherishes gold, he hates himself and he loves a woman he knows he cannot have. I must go."

"Stay with me, Lord. A little longer."

"I cannot. There is a vicious war in the Balkans. There will be many souls to receive tonight."

"Then where shall I find this key? The key beyond gold, self and a woman he cannot have?"

"I told you, Joseph. Look for another and a greater love."

FOURTEEN

THE
REVIEW OF
GAYLORD SPRIGGS

THE NEW YORK TIMES, DECEMBER 4, 1906

Well, Mr. Oscar Hammerstein's much-vaunted new Manhattan Opera House was inaugurated last night in what can only be fairly described as an unmitigated triumph. If ever another civil war was going to start again in our dear country, it must have come in the fight for seats as all New York was rocked on its heels by the spectacle we saw before us.

Exactly how much some of the great financial and cultural dynasties of our city paid for their boxes and even seats in the stalls can only be conjectured, but certainly the prices must have left the official charges out of sight.

The Manhattan, as we must now call it to differentiate from the Metropolitan across town, is a truly sumptuous building, richly ornate, with a reception area inside the doors to put to shame the rather crowded lobby afforded by the Met. And here in the half hour before the curtain rose I saw names, known only as legends across all America, milling like school-children as the lucky few were escorted to their private boxes.

There were Mellons, Vanderbilts, Rockefellers, Goulds, Whitneys and the Pierpont Morgans themselves. Present among them, genial host to us all, was the man who staked a huge fortune and limitless drive and energy to create the Manhattan against all the odds, cigar czar Oscar Hammerstein. Rumor still persists that backing Mr. H. is another and even richer tycoon, the phantom financier whom no one has ever seen, but if such a one exists he was nowhere in evidence.

The opulence of the sweeping portico and the lushness of the reception area were impressive, as was also the gilt, crimson and plum ornateness of the surprisingly small and intimate auditorium. But what of the quality of the new opera and of the singing that we had all come to hear? Both were of an artistic and emotional level that I cannot recall in thirty years.

Readers of this poor column will know that but seven weeks ago Mr. Hammerstein took the extraordinary decision to cast aside the Bellini masterpiece *I Puritani*, for his inaugural offering and instead undertake the frightening risk of introducing a completely new opera in the modern style by an unknown (and amazingly still anonymous) American composer. What an extraordinary gamble. Did it pay off? One thousand percent.

Firstly, *The Angel of Shiloh* secured the presence of Vicomtesse Christine de Chagny of Paris, a beauty with a voice that last night eclipsed any in my memory, and I believe I have heard the best in the world over these past thirty years. Secondly, the work itself is a masterpiece of simplicity and emotion that left not a dry eye in the house.

The story is set in our own Civil War of only forty years ago and is therefore of immediate significance to any American of North or South. In Act One we meet the dashing young Connecticut lawyer Miles Regan, hopelessly in love with Eugenie Delarue, the beautiful daughter of a wealthy plantation owner of Virginia. The former role was taken by rising American tenor David Melrose until something most strange occurred— but more of this anon. The couple duly plight their troth and exchange golden rings. As the Southern belle Mme. de Chagny was magnificent and her simple girlish pleasure at the proposal of the man she loves, expressed in the aria "With this ring forever," communicated that delight to the whole audience.

The neighboring plantation owner, Joshua Howard, magnificently sung by Alessandro Gonci, has also been the suitor for her hand in marriage but accepts his rejection and heartbreak like the gentleman he is. But the clouds of war are looming and at the end of the act the first guns fire on Fort Sumter, and the Union is at war with the Confederacy. The young lovers have to part. Regan explains that he has no choice but to return to Connecticut and fight for the North. Miss Delarue knows she must stay with her family, all dedicated to the South. The act ends with one heartrending duet as the lovers part, not knowing if they will ever meet again.

For Act Two, two years have passed and Eugenie Delarue has volunteered as a nurse in a hospital just after the bloody Battle of Shiloh. We see her selfless devotion to the terribly injured young men in the uniforms of both sides as they are brought in, a formerly sheltered plantation belle now exposed to all the filth and pain of a front-line hospital. In a single and utterly moving aria she asks "Why must these young men die?"

Her former neighbor and suitor is now Colonel Howard, commanding the regiment occupying the site of the hospital. He resumes his courtship, seeking to persuade her to forget her lost fiancé in the Union Army and accept him instead. She is half decided so to do when a new arrival is brought in. He is a Union officer, terribly injured when a powder magazine exploded in his face. This face is swathed in surgical gauze, clearly ruined beyond repair. Even as he remains unconscious Miss Delarue recognizes the gold ring upon one finger, the same ring she offered two years ago. The tragic officer is indeed Captain Regan, still sung by David Melrose. When he awakes, he quickly recognizes his fiancée but does not realize that he himself has been recognized while asleep. There is a supremely ironic scene in which, from his bed and helpless, he witnesses Colonel Howard enter the ward to press his suit yet again with Miss Delarue, trying to convince her that her lover must by now be dead, when she and we know that he lies a few feet away. This act ends when Captain Regan perceives that she knows who he is behind the bandages and, seeing himself for the first time in a mirror, realizes that the once handsome face is now a ruin. He seeks to snatch a revolver from a guard and end his own life, but the Confederate soldier and two Union prisoner/patients restrain him.

The third act is the climax and deeply moving it turns out to be. For Colonel Howard announces that to his new knowledge Eugenie's former fiancé is none other than the leader of the fearsome Regan's Raiders, who have carried out devastating ambushes behind the lines. As such he will, upon capture, be subjected to a drumhead court-martial and shot.

Eugenie Delarue is now in a terrible dilemma. Should she betray the Confederacy by keeping her knowledge to herself, or denounce the man she still loves? At this point a brief armistice is announced to enable an exchange of prisoners deemed permanently hors de combat. The man with the destroyed face qualifies for inclusion in the exchange; covered wagons arrive with wounded Confederate soldiers from the North, to pick up their own crippled soldiers in the hands of the South.

At this point I must describe the amazing events that happened backstage during the entr'acte. It seems (and my source is quite certain of this) that Mr. Melrose sprayed a soothing linctus upon his throat to ease the larynx. It must have been contaminated in some way, for within seconds he was croaking like a frog. Disaster!! The curtain was about to rise. Then appeared an understudy, miraculously made up for the part. His face swathed in bandages, just in time to step into the breach.

Normally this would have been a terrible disappointment for the audience. But in this case all the gods of opera must have been smiling upon Mr. Hammerstein. The understudy, unlisted in the program and still unknown to me, sang in a tenor to match that of the great Signor Gonci himself.

Miss Delarue decided that as Captain Regan would never fight again she had no need to reveal what she knew of the man in the mask. As the wagons prepared to roll north Colonel Howard learned that somewhere the wanted leader of Regan's Raiders had been injured and was presumably behind Confederate lines. Notices offering a reward for his capture were posted. Every Union soldier leaving for the North was compared with a sketch of Regan's face. To no avail. For by now Captain Regan has no face.

As the soldiers destined to be repatriated to the

North wait through the night for their dawn departure, we are treated to a most charming interlude. Colonel Howard, the great Gonci himself, has throughout the action been attended by a young aide-de-camp, no more than a boy of perhaps thirteen. Until this point he has uttered no sound. But as one of the Union soldiers tries to coax a tune out of his soldier's fiddle the boy quietly takes the instrument from him and plays a beautiful melody as if he were handling a Stradivarius. One of the wounded men asks if he can sing the song of the tune; in answer the boy lays aside the fiddle and gives us an aria in a treble of such sweet clarity that I know it brought a lump to the throat of almost everyone present. And when I studied my program for his name, lo! he turned out to be none other than Master Pierre de Chagny, son of the diva herself. So, a chip off the old block.

In the parting scene of quite exquisite pathos Miss Delarue and her Unionist fiancé say their farewells. Mme. de Chagny had already sung throughout with a purity of voice normally ascribed only to angels. But now she rose to new and seemingly unattainable heights of vocal beauty, the like of which I have never heard. As she began the aria "Will we never meet again?" she seemed to be singing her heart out, and as the unknown understudy returned the ring she had given him with the words "Take back this band" I saw a thousand squares of cambric fly to the faces of the ladies of New York.

It was an evening that will remain in the hearts and

minds of any who were there. I swear I saw the normally fiercely disciplined Maestro Campanini almost in
tears as Mme. de Chagny, alone on the stage and lit
only by candle lamps in the darkened hospital ward,
brought the opera to a close with "Oh, Cruel War."

There were thirty-seven standing ovations and curtain calls, and that was before I had to leave to find
out what had happened to Mr. Melrose and his throat
linctus. Alas, he had left in tears.

While the rest of the company was superb and the
orchestra under Signor Campanini nothing less than
one would expect, the night must belong to the young
lady from Paris. Her beauty and charm already have
the entire staff at the Waldorf-Astoria literally at her
feet and now the unalloyed magic of that voice has
conquered every opera-lover who had the good fortune
to be at the Manhattan last night.

What a tragedy that she must depart so soon. She
will sing for us for another five evenings and must then
depart for Europe to fulfill previous engagements at
Covent Garden before Christmas. Her place will be
taken early next month by Dame Nellie Melba, Oscar
Hammerstein's second triumph over his crosstown rivals. She too is a legend in her lifetime, and she too
will be singing her New York debut, but she must look
to her laurels, for no one who was present last night
will ever forget La Divina.

And what of the Metropolitan? Among the great
dynasts whose wealth backs the Met I think I noted,
mixed with their delight at the new masterpiece, some

sharp glances to each other as if to ask: what now? Clearly, despite its smaller auditorium, the Manhattan has finer front-of-house facilities, a huge stage, the very latest technology and deeply impressive sets. If Mr. Hammerstein can continue to offer us the quality we saw last night the Met will have to dig deep to match him.

FIFTEEN

THE
REPORT OF
AMY FONTAINE

SOCIETY COLUMN, *NEW YORK WORLD*,
DECEMBER 4, 1906

Well, there are parties and there are parties, but surely the one held last night at the new Manhattan Opera House following the triumphal rendition of *The Angel of Shiloh* must rank as the party of this decade.

Attending as I do on behalf of *World* readers nearly a thousand social events a year, I can still truly say I have never seen so many celebrated Americans under one roof.

When the last and final curtain came down after ovations and curtain-calls too numerous to count, the glittering audience began to drift towards the great West Thirty-fourth Street portico where a jam of carriages awaited them. These were the unfortunates not coming to the party itself. Those in the audience with invitations tarried until the curtain went up again, then walked up the hastily erected ramp over the orchestra pit and up to the stage. Others who had not been able to make the performance came in through the stage door.

Our host for the evening was tobacco magnate Mr. Oscar Hammerstein, who has designed, built and owns the Manhattan Opera House. He took center stage and personally welcomed each guest coming from the auditorium. Among them were surely every name even remotely associated with New York, prominent among them the *World's* proprietor, Mr. Joseph Pulitzer.

The stage itself formed a magnificent backdrop to the party, for Mr. Hammerstein had retained the Southern mansion that features in the opera, so that we were gathering under its very walls. Round the perimeter, stagehands had quickly placed a range of genuine antique tables, which groaned with food and drink, with a lively bar and six tenders to ensure no one went thirsty.

Mayor George McClellan was quickly there, mingling with Rockefellers and Vanderbilts as the crowd swelled and swelled. The whole party was in honor of the young prima donna Vicomtesse Christine de Chagny who had just established such a magnificent triumph on that very stage, and the most notable people of New York could hardly wait to meet her. At the start she was resting in her dressing room, bombarded with messages of congratulation, bouquets of flowers so

numerous that they had to be sent down to the Bellevue Hospital at her personal request, and invitations
to the greatest houses in the city.

Moving through the growing crowd I sought out
people whose exploits might fascinate readers of the
New York World and came across two young actors,
D.W. Griffith and Mr. Douglas Fairbanks, in earnest
conversation. Mr. Griffith, fresh from playing in Boston, informed me he was toying with the notion of
leaving New England for a sunny village outside Los
Angeles, where he was interested in a (crazy-sounding)
new form of entertainment call "biographs." Apparently these involve moving images on a strip of
celluloid. I heard Mr. Fairbanks laughingly tell his fellow thespian that when he became a star on Broadway
he might follow him to Hollywood, but only if anything ever became of the biographs. At this point a
tall marine emerged from the portico of the mansion
and announced in a loud voice: "Ladies and Gentlemen, the President of the United States."

I could hardly believe my ears, but it was true, and
in seconds there he was, President Teddy Roosevelt,
eyeglasses perched on his nose, beaming his cheery grin
and moving through the crowd shaking hands with
everyone. Nor had he come alone, for he has a de-
served reputation for surrounding himself with the
most colorful characters from our society. Within
minutes I found my poor hand gripped in the giant fist
of former heavyweight champion of the world Bob Fitzsimmons, while standing a few yards away were another

former champion, Sailor Tom Sharkey and the reigning champ, Canadian Tommy Burns. I felt a midget among these towering men.

At that moment there appeared in the doorway of the mansion the star herself. She descended to a rapturous round of applause led by the President, who advanced to be introduced by Mr. Hammerstein. With Old World gallantry Mr. Roosevelt took her hand and kissed it, to a cheer from the assembled throng. Then he greeted chief tenor Signor Gonci and the rest of the cast as Mr. Hammerstein introduced them.

With the formalities over our roguish chief executive took the lovely young French aristocrat on his arm and escorted her round the room to introduce her to those he knew.

Moving closer to the presidential entourage I heard Teddy Roosevelt introduce Mme. de Chagny to his niece's new husband and soon found a chance to have a few words with this startlingly handsome young man. He is just down from Harvard and studying at the Columbia Law School. Of course I asked him if he contemplated a career in politics like his famous uncle and he conceded that he might one day.

With the party livening up, the food and drink circulating merrily, I noted that a piano had been positioned in one corner with a young man at the keyboard producing light-hearted music of our era in contrast to the more serious classical arias of the opera. He turned out to be a young Russian immigrant, still with a strong accent, who told me he had composed some of the airs he was playing himself and wished to become an established composer. Well, good luck, Irving Berlin.

In the early part of the festivities there seemed to be one person missing whom many would have liked to meet and congratulate—the unknown understudy who had taken over the role of the hospitalized David Melrose as the tragic Captain Regan. At first one thought his absence could be explained by the difficulty of removing the considerable makeup that covered most of his face. The rest of the cast was circulating freely, a pageant of dark blue-and-gold Union uniforms with the dove gray coats of the Confederate soldiers. But even those who had been playing the wounded soldiers of the hospital scenes had speedily removed their bandages and thrown away their rough crutches. And still the mysterious tenor was missing.

His appearance, when he came, was in the main doorway of the plantation house, atop the double stairway leading down to the stage where we were all enjoying the party. And what a brief appearance it was! Is this extraordinarily talented singer really that shy? Many of those below the portico missed him completely. But there was one who did not.

As he came through the doorway I saw that he had still retained his heavy makeup, the bandage that covered most of his face in the opera, allowing only his eyes to show, and a line of the jaw. He had his hand on the shoulder of the young treble who had so entranced us with his singing, Pierre, the son of Mme. de

Chagny. He seemed to be whispering in the boy's ear and the child was nodding in understanding.

Mme. de Chagny saw them at once and it seemed to me a shadow of fear passed over her face. Her eyes locked on those behind the mask, she went very pale, noticed her son beside the tenor in the Union blue and her hand flew to her mouth. Then she was running up the staircase towards the strange apparition, while the music played on and the crowd roared in conversation and laughter.

I saw the two speak intently to each other for several moments. Mme. de Chagny took the tenor's hand off her son's shoulder and gestured the boy to run down the stairs, which he did, no doubt seeking a well-deserved soda pop. Only then did the diva suddenly laugh and smile, as if in relief. Was he complimenting her on the performance of a lifetime or did she seem to fear for the boy?

Finally I noticed him pass her a message, a slip of paper, which she palmed and put inside her bodice. Then he was gone, back through the mansion door, and the prima donna descended the stairwell alone to rejoin the party. I do not think anyone else noticed this most strange incident.

It was well after midnight when the revelers, tired but extremely happy, departed for their carriages, their hotels and their homes. I, of course, hurried back to the offices of the *New York World* to ensure that you, my dear readers, would be the first to know what happened last night at the Manhattan Opera House.

SIXTEEN

LECTURE OF
PROF. CHARLES BLOOM

School of Journalism, Columbia University,
New York, March 1947

Ladies and gentlemen, young Americans striving one day to be great journalists, since we have never met before let me introduce myself. My name is Charles Bloom. I have been a working journalist, mainly in this city, for almost fifty years.

I began around the turn of the century as a copy boy in the offices of the old *New York American* and by 1903 had persuaded the paper to raise me to the lofty status, or so it seemed to me, of general reporter on the city desk, covering all the newsworthy events of this city on a daily basis.

Over the years I have witnessed and covered many, many news stories; some heroic, some momentous, some which changed the course of our and the world's history, some simply tragic. I was there to cover the lonely departure of Charles Lindbergh from a mist-shrouded field when he set off across the Atlantic and I was there to welcome back a global hero. I covered the inauguration of Franklin D. Roosevelt and the news of his death two years ago. I never went to Europe in the First World War but saw off the doughboys when they left this harbor for the fields of Flanders.

I moved from the *American*, where I had intimately known a colleague called Damon Runyon, to the *Herald Tribune* and finally the *Times*.

I have covered murders and suicides, Mafia gang wars and mayoral elections, wars and the treaties that ended them, visiting celebrities and the denizens of Skid Row. I have lived with the high and the mighty, the poor and the destitute, covered the doings of the great and the good and those of the mean and the vicious. And all in this one single city, which never dies and never sleeps.

During the last war, though a bit long in the tooth, I arranged to be sent to Europe, flew with our B17s over Germany—which I have to tell you scared the hell out of me—witnessed the German surrender almost two years ago and as my final assignment covered the Potsdam Conference in the summer of '45. There I met the British leader Winston Churchill, to be voted out of office right in mid-conference and replaced by their new premier Clement Attlee; and our own President Truman of course, and even Marshal

Stalin, a man who I fear will soon cease to be our friend and become very much our enemy.

On my return I was due for retirement, elected to go before I was pushed, and received a kind offer from the chairman of this department to join as a visiting professor and try to impart to you some of the things I have learned the hard way.

If anyone were to ask me what qualities make a good journalist, I would say there are four. First, you should always try not simply to see, to witness and to report, but to understand. Try to understand the people you are meeting, the events you are seeing. There is an old saying: To understand everything is to forgive everything. Man cannot understand everything because he is flawed, but he can try. So we seek to report back what really happened to those who were not there but wish to know. For in future time history will record that we were the witnesses; that we saw more of it than the politicians, civil servants, bankers, financiers, tycoons and generals. Because they were locked in their separate worlds, but we were everywhere. And if we witnessed badly, without understanding what we were seeing and hearing, we will only notate a series of facts and figures, giving as great credence to the lies we are always being told as to the truth, and thus creating a false picture.

Secondly, never stop learning. There is no end to the process. Be like a squirrel. Store pieces of information and insight that come your way; you never know when that tiny piece of intelligence will be the clinching explanation to a jigsaw of the otherwise unexplainable.

Thirdly, you have to develop a "nose" for a story. Meaning a kind of sixth sense, an awareness that something is not quite right, that there is something odd going on and no one else can see it. If you never develop this nose, you will perhaps be competent and conscientious, a credit to the job. But stories will pass you by unsuspected; you will attend the official briefings and be told what the powers that be want you to know. You will report faithfully what they said, false or true. You will take your paycheck and go home, a good job well done. But you will not, without the nose, ever stroll into the bar on an adrenalin high knowing that you have just blown apart the biggest scandal of the year because you noticed something odd in a chance remark, a column of doctored figures, an unjustified acquittal, a suddenly dropped charge, and all your colleagues failed to spot it. There is in our job nothing quite like that adrenalin high; it is like winning a Grand Prix race, to know that you have just filed a major exclusive and blown the competing media to hell.

We journalists are never destined to be loved. Like cops, this is something we just have to accept if we want to take up our strange career. But, though they may not like us, the high and the mighty need us.

The movie star may push us aside as he stalks to his limousine, but if the press fails to mention him or his movies, fails to print his picture or monitor his comings and goings for a couple of months, his agent is soon screaming for attention.

The politician may denounce us when he is in power, but try ignoring him totally when he is running for election or has some self-praising triumph to announce and he will plead for some coverage.

It pleases the high and the mighty to look down on the press but, boy, do they need us. For they live on and off the publicity that only we can give them. The sports stars want their performances to be reported, as the sports fans want to know. The society hostesses direct us to the tradesman's entrance but if we ignore their charity balls and their social conquests they are distraught.

Journalism is a form of power. Badly used, power is a tyranny; well and carefully used it is a requirement without which no society can survive and prosper. But that brings us to rule four: it is not our job ever to join the Establishment, to pretend that we have, by close juxtaposition, actually joined the high and the mighty. Our job in a democracy is to probe, to uncover, to check, to expose, to unveil, to question, to interrogate. Our job is to disbelieve, until that which we are being told can be proved to be true. Because we have power, we are besieged by the mountebanks, the phonies, the charlatans, the snake-oil salesmen—in finance, commerce, industry, showbiz and above all politics.

Your masters must be Truth and the reader, no one else. Never fawn, never cower, never be bullied into submission and never forget that the reader with his dime has as much right to your effort and your respect, as much right to hear the truth as the Senate. Remain therefore skeptical in the face of power and privilege and you will do us all credit.

And now, because the hour is late and you are no doubt tired of study, I will fill what remains of this period by telling a story. A story about a story. And no, it is not a story in which I was the triumphant hero, but just the opposite. It was a story that I failed to see unraveling all around me because I was young and brash and I failed to understand what I was really witnessing.

It was also a story, the only one in my life, that I never wrote up. I never filed it though the archives do retain the basic outlines that were released eventually to the press by the police department. But I was there; I saw it all, I ought to have known but I failed to spot it. That was partly why I never filed it. But also partly because there are some things that happen to people which, if exposed to the world, will destroy them. Some deserve it and I have met them: Nazi generals, Mafia bosses, corrupt labor leaders and venal politicians. But most people do not deserve to be destroyed and the lives of some are already so tragic that exposure of their misery would only double their pain. All this for a few column inches to wrap tomorrow's fish? Maybe, but even though I then worked for Randolph Hearst's yellow press and would have been fired if the editor had ever found out, what I saw was too sad for me to file and I let it go. Now, forty years on, it matters not much anymore.

It was in the winter of 1906. I was twenty-four, a New York street kid proud to be a reporter on the *American* and loving it. When I look back at what I was I stand amazed at my own impudence. I was brash, full of myself, but understood very little.

That December the city was playing host to one of the most famous opera singers in the world, a certain Christine de Chagny. She had come to star in the opening week of a new opera house, the Manhattan Opera, which went out of business three years later. She was thirty-two, beautiful and very charming. She had brought her twelve-year-old son, Pierre, along with a maid and the boy's tutor, an Irish priest called Father Joseph Kilfoyle. Plus two male secretaries. She arrived without her husband six days before her inaugural appearance at the opera house on December third and her husband joined her on a later ship on the second, having been detained by the affairs of his estates in Normandy.

Though I knew nothing of opera, her appearance caused a major stir because no singer of her eminence had till then crossed the Atlantic to star in New York. She was the toast of the town. By a combination of luck and good old-fashioned chutzpah I had managed to persuade her to allow me to be her guide to New York and its various sights and spectacles. It was a dream of an assignment. She was so hounded by the press that her host, the opera impresario Oscar Hammerstein, had forbidden all access to her before the gala opening. Yet here was I, with access to her suite at the Waldorf-Astoria, able to file daily bulletins on her itinerary and engagements. Thanks to this my career on the *American* city desk was taking off by leaps and bounds.

Yet there was something mysterious and strange going on all around us and I failed to spot it. The "something" involved a bizarre and elusive figure who seemed to appear and disappear at will and yet who clearly was playing some kind of role behind the scenes.

First there had been a letter, brought personally by the hand of a lawyer from Paris, France. By a complete coincidence I had helped deliver that letter to the headquarters of one of the richest and most powerful corporations in New York. There, in the boardroom, I caught a fleeting glimpse of the man behind the corporation, the one to whom the letter was addressed. He was staring at me from a spyhole in the wall, a terrifying face covered in a mask. I thought little more about it, and no one believed me anyway.

Within four weeks the prima donna scheduled for the inaugural gala of the Manhattan Opera had been canceled and the French diva invited over at an astronomical fee. From Paris, France. Rumors also started that Oscar Hammerstein had a secret and even richer backer, an invisible financier /partner who had ordered him to make the change. I should have suspected the connection, but did not.

On the day the lady arrived at the quayside on the Hudson, the strange phantom appeared again. This time I did not see him, but a colleague did. The description was identical, a lone figure in a mask, standing atop a warehouse watching the prima donna from Paris arrive in New York. Again I failed to see the connection. Later it was obvious that he had sent for her, overruling Hammerstein. But why? I found out eventually but by then it was too late.

As I said, I met the lady, she seemed to like me and allowed me into her suite for an exclusive interview. There her son unwrapped an anonymous present, a music box in the form of a monkey. When Mme. de Chagny heard the tune it played she looked as if she had been struck by lightning. She whispered, " 'Masquerade.' Twelve years ago. He must be here," and still for me the light refused to go on.

She was desperate to trace the source of the monkey-doll, and I figured it must have come from a toy shop at Coney Island. Two days later we all went there, with me acting as guide to the party. Again, something very strange happened and once again no alarm bells rang.

The party consisted of me; the prima donna; her son, Pierre; and his tutor, Father Joe Kilfoyle.

Because I had no interest in the toys, I handed Mme. de Chagny and her son over to the care of the fun master, who was in overall charge of the fair. I did not bother to enter the toy shop myself. I should have done, for I learned later that the man showing the child and his mother around was none other than a most sinister figure calling himself Darius, whom I had seen weeks earlier while delivering the letter from Paris. Later I learned from the fun master, who was present throughout, that this man had offered his services as an expert on toys, but in truth spent his time quietly interrogating the boy about his parentage.

Anyway, I walked by the sea's edge with the Catholic priest while the boy and his mother examined the toys inside the shop. It seems there were racks of these monkey toys, but not one played the strange tune I had heard the first one play in her suite at the Waldorf-Astoria.

Then she went off with the fun master to examine a place called the Hall of Mirrors. Again, I did not go in. Anyway, I was not invited. Finally I returned to the fair to see if the party was ready to leave and return to Manhattan.

I saw the Irish priest escorting the boy back to the coach we had hired at the train station and noticed but only vaguely that another coach was almost beside it. That was odd because the place was deserted.

I was halfway between the gate and the Hall of Mirrors when a figure appeared, racing towards me in what seemed like a panic. It was Darius. He was the chief executive officer of the corporation whose real boss seemed to be the mysterious man in the mask. I thought he was running at me, but he raced straight past me as if I were not there. He was coming from the Hall of Mirrors. As he passed me he shouted something, not to me but as if to the sea wind. I could not understand it. It was not in English, but having a good ear for sounds if not always their meaning, I took my pencil and scribbled down what I thought I had heard.

Later, much later and too late, I returned to Coney Island and spoke again with the fun master, who showed me a journal he kept in which he had noted down all that occurred inside the Hall of Mirrors while I was walking on the beach. If only I had seen that passage I could have understood what was happening around me and done something to prevent what came later. But I did not see inside the fun master's journal, and I did not understand three words in Latin.

Now, it may seem strange to you young people but in those days dress was pretty formal. Young men were expected to wear dark suits at all times, often with a vest, plus stiff starched white collars and cuffs. The trouble was, that posed a laundry bill that young men on meager salaries could not afford. So many of us wore detachable white celluloid collars and cuffs, which could be taken off at night and wiped clean with a damp cloth. This enabled a shirt to be worn for several days, but always exposing a clean collar and cuffs. With my notebook in my jacket pocket, I wrote down the words shouted by the man I knew only as Darius on my left cuff.

He seemed half-crazy as he ran past me, quite different from the ice-cold executive I had met in the boardroom. His black eyes were wide open and staring, his face still white as a skull, his jet-black hair flying in the wind as he ran. I turned to follow his progress and saw him reach the park gate. There he met the Irish priest, who had shut the boy, Pierre, in the coach and was coming back to look for his employer.

Darius stopped on seeing the priest and the two of them stared at each other for several seconds. Even across thirty yards of November wind I could sense the tension. They were like two pit bulls meeting the day before the fight. Then Darius broke away, ran for his own coach and drove off.

Father Kilfoyle came up the path looking grim and thoughtful. Mme. de Chagny emerged from the Hall of Mirrors pale and shaken. I was in the midst of one hell of a drama and could not understand what I was witnessing. We drove back to the El train station and then by train to Manhattan in silence, except the boy who chattered happily to me about the toy shop.

My last clue came three days later. The inaugural gala was a triumph, a new opera whose name escapes me, but then I never did turn into an opera buff. Apparently Mme. de Chagny sang like an angel from heaven and left half the audience in tears. Later there was a hell of a party right on the stage. President Teddy Roosevelt was there with all the mega-rich of New York society; there were boxers, Buffalo Bill—yes, young lady, I really met him—and all paying court to the young opera star.

The opera had been set in the American Civil War and the principal set was the front of a magnificent Virginian plantation house with a front door raised up and steps leading down each side to the stage level. Halfway through the celebration party a man appeared in the doorway.

I recognized him at once, or thought I did. He was dressed in the costume of his part, the uniform of a wounded captain of the Union forces but one who had been so badly wounded in the head that most of his face was covered by a mask. It was he who had sung a passionate duet with Mme. de Chagny in the final act, when he gave her back their betrothal ring. Strangely, considering the opera was over, he still wore his mask. Then I finally realized why. This *was* the Phantom, the elusive figure who seemed to own so much of New York, who had helped create the Manhattan Opera House with his money and had brought the French aristocrat over the Atlantic to sing. But why? This I did not learn until later, and too late.

I was talking with Vicomte de Chagny at the time, a charming man incredibly proud of his wife's success and delighted that he had just met our president. Over his shoulder I saw the prima donna go up the staircase to the portico and talk with the figure I had then begun to think of as the Phantom. I knew it was he again. It could be no one else, and he seemed to have some kind of a hold over her. I had not yet worked out that they had known each other, twelve years earlier, in Paris, and much much more besides.

Before they parted, he palmed her a small note on folded paper, which she slipped inside her bodice. Then he was gone again, as always; there one second and disappeared the next.

There was a gossip columnist from a rival paper, the *New York World*, a Pulitzer rag, and she wrote the next day that she had seen the incident but thought no one else had. She was wrong. I did. But more. I kept an eye on the lady for the rest of the evening and sure enough, after a while she turned away from the gathering, opened the note and read it. When she had done she glanced around, screwed the paper into a ball and threw it into one of the trash cans placed to receive empty bottles and dirty napkins. A few moments later I retrieved it. And, just in case you young people might be interested, I have it here today.

That night I simply stuffed it into my pocket. It lay for a week on the dressing table in my small apartment and later I kept it as the only memento I will ever have of the events that took place before my eyes. It says: "Let me see the boy just once. Let me say one last farewell. Please. The day you sail away. Dawn. Battery Park. Erik."

Then and only then did I put some of it together. The secret admirer before her marriage, twelve years earlier in Paris. The unrequited love who had emigrated to America and become rich and powerful enough to arrange for her to come and star in his own opera house. Touching stuff, but more for your romantic lady novelist than a hard-bitten reporter on the streets of New York, for such I thought myself to be. But why was he masked? Why not come and meet her like everyone else? To these I still had no answers. Nor did I seek any, and that was my mistake.

Anyway, the lady sang for six nights. Each time she brought the house down. December eighth was her last performance. Another prima donna, Dame Nellie Melba, the world's only rival to the French aristocrat, was due to sail in on the twelfth. Mme. de Chagny, her husband, son and accompanying party, would board the RMS *City of Paris*, bound for Southampton, England, to take over at Covent Garden. Their departure was scheduled for December tenth and for all the friendship she had shown me I was determined to be there on the Hudson to see her off. By this time I was virtually accepted by all her entourage as one of the family. In the private send-off in her stateroom I would get my last exclusive for the *New York American*. Then I would go back to covering the doings of murderers, the bulls and the bosses of Tammany Hall.

The night of the ninth I slept badly. I do not know why, but you will all understand there are such nights, and after a certain time you know there is no point in trying to get to sleep again. Better to get up and have done with it. This I did at 5:00 A.M. I washed and shaved, then dressed in my best dark suit. I fixed my stiff collar with back stud and front stud and knotted my tie. Without thinking I picked two stiff white plastic cuffs from the half dozen on the dressing-table and slipped them on. As I was awake so early I thought I

might as well go across to the Waldorf-Astoria and join
the de Chagny party for breakfast. To save a cab fare
I walked, arriving at ten before seven. It was still dark,
but in the breakfast room Father Kilfoyle was sitting
alone with a coffee. He greeted me cheerily and beckoned me over.

"Ah, Mr. Bloom," he said, "so, we must be leaving
your fine city. Come to see us off, have you? Well, good
for you. But some hot porridge and toast will set you
up for the day. Waiter . . ." Soon the vicomte himself
joined us and he and the priest exchanged a few words
in French. I could not follow them, but asked if the
vicomtesse and Pierre would be joining us. Father Kilfoyle indicated the vicomte and told me Madame had
gone to Pierre's room to get him ready, which was apparently what he had just learned, but in French. I
thought I knew better, but said nothing. It was a private matter and nothing to do with me if the lady
wished to slip away to say farewell to her strange spon-
sor. I expected that about eight o'clock she would
come rattling up to the doors in a hansom cab and
greet us with her usual winning smile and charming
manners.

So we sat, the three of us, and to make conversation
I asked the priest if he had enjoyed New York. Very
much, he said, a fine city and full of his compatriots.
And Coney Island, I asked. At this he became grim.
A strange place, he said at last, with some strange people on it. The fun master, I asked. Him . . . and others,
he said.

Still the innocent abroad, I blundered on. Oh, you mean Darius, I said. At once he spun round upon me, his blue eyes boring like gimlets. "How do you know him?" he asked. "I met him once before," I replied. "Tell me where and when," he said, and it was more like an order than a request. But the affair of the letter seemed harmless enough so I explained what had happened between me and the Parisian lawyer, Dufour, and of our visit to the penthouse suite at the top of the city's highest tower. It simply never occurred to me that Father Kilfoyle, apart from being the boy's tutor, was also the father confessor to both vicomte and vicomtesse.

Sometime during this Vicomte de Chagny, evidently bored by his lack of understanding of English, had excused himself and gone back upstairs. I continued with my narrative, explaining that I had been surprised when Darius ran past me, looking distraught, shouting three incomprehensible words. He had his brief eyeball confrontation with Father Kilfoyle and then had driven off. The priest listened in frowning silence, then asked: Do you remember what he said?" I explained it was in a foreign language, but that I had jotted down what I thought I had heard on, of all places, my left plastic cuff.

At this point M. de Chagny came back. He seemed worried, and spoke rapidly in French to Father Kilfoyle, who translated for me. "They are not there. Mother and son are not to be found." Of course, I knew why, and tried to be reassuring by saying, "Don't worry. They have gone out to a meeting."

The priest stared at me hard, forgetting to ask how I knew, but simply repeated the word, "Meeting?" "Just to say good-bye to an old friend, a Mr. Erik," I added, still trying to be helpful. The Irishman kept staring at me and then seemed to recall what we had been talking about before the vicomte returned to us. He reached across, grabbed my left forearm, pulled it towards him and turned it over.

And there they were, the three words in pencil. For ten days that cuff had lain among others on my dressing table and that morning I had by chance grabbed it again and slipped it over my wrist. Father Kilfoyle gave the cuff one glance and let out a single word that I never knew Catholic priests were aware of, let alone used. But *he* did. Then he was up, dragging me out of my chair by the throat, shouting into my face, "Where in God's name did she go?" "Battery Park," I croaked.

He was off, racing to the lobby, with me and the hapless vicomte running along behind him. Through the main doors he went, and found a brougham under the marquee with a top-hatted gentleman about to climb in. The poor man was seized by the jacket and hurled aside as the man in the cassock leaped inside, shouting to the coachman, "Battery Park. Drive like the devil himself." I was just in time to jump in after, and hauled the poor Frenchman after me as the carriage hit the road.

All through the drive Father Kilfoyle was hunched in his seat in the corner, hands clasping the cross on the chain round his neck. He was furiously murmuring, "Holy Mary, Mother of God, grant that we may be in time." At one point he paused and I leaned across, pointing to the pencil marks on my cuff. "What do they mean?" I asked. He seemed to take some time to focus on my face.

" *'Delenda Est Filius'* " he replied, repeating the words I had written down. "They mean: 'The son must be destroyed.' " I leaned back, feeling sick.

It was not the prima donna who was in danger from the crazed man who had run past me at Coney Island, but her son. But still there was a mystery. Why would Darius, obsessed though he might be at the thought of inheriting his master's fortune, want to kill the harmless son of the French couple? The carriage raced on down an almost empty Broadway, and over to the east, beyond Brooklyn, the dawn began to pink the sky. We arrived at the main gate on State Street and the priest was out and running into the park.

Now, Battery Park then was not as it is now. Today vagrants and derelicts adorn the lawns. Then it was a quiet and placid place with a network of paths and walkways spreading out from Castle Clinton, and among them recesses and arbors with stone benches, in any one of which we might find the people we were looking for.

Outside the gate of the park I noticed three separate carriages. One was a closed brougham in the livery of the Waldorf-Astoria itself, clearly the one that had brought the vicomtesse and her son. The coachman sat on his box, huddled against the cold. The second was another of equal size, but unmarked, nevertheless of a style and state of repair that would be owned by a wealthy man or corporation.

Parked some distance farther on was a small carriage, the self-drive calash that I had seen ten days earlier outside the funfair grounds. Clearly Darius had arrived too, and there was no time to waste. We all ran full tilt through the park's gateway.

Inside the park we split up, running in different directions the better to cover more ground. It was still dusky among the trees and hedges and hard to make out human forms as opposed to the many bushes. But after several minutes running hither and thither I heard voices, one manly, deep and musical, the other that of the beautiful opera singer. I wondered whether to turn away to find the others or to approach. In fact I crept quietly nearer, until I was behind a block of privet hedge fringing a clearing among the trees.

I should have run forward at once, made my presence known and shouted a warning. But the boy was not there. For one optimistic moment I thought the vicomtesse might still have left him at the hotel after all. So I paused to listen. The two stood at each side of the clearing but their low voices carried easily to where I crouched behind the hedge.

The man was masked as ever but I knew when I saw him that it was he who had been the Union officer who had sung that amazing duet with the prima donna at the opera house and brought the audience to tears. The voice was the same, but this was the first time I had ever heard it speaking.

"Where is Pierre?" he asked.

"He is in the coach still," she replied. "I asked him to give us a few moments. He will come shortly."

My heart leaped. If the boy was in the coach there was a good chance that Darius, hunting somewhere in the park, would not find him.

"What do you want of me?" she asked the Phantom.

"All my life I have been rejected and rebuffed, treated with cruelty and mockery. Why . . . you know too well. Just once, all those years ago, I thought for one fleeting hour that I might have found love. Something bigger and warmer than the endless bitterness of existence. . . ."

"Stop, Erik. It could not be, it cannot be. Once I thought you were a real ghost, my invisible Angel of Music. Later I learned the truth, that you were a man in every sense. Then I came to fear you, your power, your sometimes savage anger, your genius. But even with the fear was a compulsive fascination like a rabbit before the cobra.

"That last evening, in the darkness by the lake far beneath the Opera I was so afraid I thought I would die of fear. I was half swooning when what happened . . . happened. When you spared me and Raoul and vanished again into the shadows, I believed I would never see you again. Then I understood better all you had been through and felt only compassion and tenderness for my fearsome outcast.

"But love, true love, anything to match that passion you felt for me . . . this I could not feel. Better you should have hated me."

"Never hate, Christine. Only love. I loved you then and ever since and always will. But now I accept. The wound is cauterized at last. There is another love. My son. Our son. What will you tell him of me?"

"That he has a friend, a true and dear friend, here in America. In five years I will tell him the truth. That you are his real father. And he will choose. If he can accept this, that Raoul has been everything for him that a father can be, and done everything for him that a father can do, and yet is not his real parent—then he will come to you and with my blessing."

I found myself rooted behind the hedge, stunned by what I had heard. Suddenly everything that had drifted by me unobserved and not understood became too clear. The letter from Paris that had told this strange hermit of a man that he had a son alive, the secret plan to bring mother and child to New York, the secret tryst to see them both, and most terrible of all, the crazed hatred of Darius against the boy who would now displace him as the heir of the multimillionaire.

Darius . . . I suddenly recalled that he too was some-where among the shadows and was about to throw my-self forward with the too-long-delayed warning. Then I heard the approaching feet of the others to my right. At this point the sun rose, flooding the glade with a pink light, turning to rose the dusting of snow that had fallen in the night. Then three figures came into view.

From separate paths to my right the vicomte and the priest appeared. Both stopped in their tracks when they saw the man in the sweeping cape, the wide-brimmed hat and the mask that always covered his face, talking to Mme. de Chagny. I heard the vicomte whisper: "Le Fantôme." To my left the boy, Pierre, came running. Even as he did so, there was a low click close to me. I turned.

Between two large bushes, not ten yards away, almost invisible among the remaining deep shadows, was the crouching figure of a man. He was all in black but I caught a glimpse of a bone-white face and of something in his right hand with a long barrel. I drew in air and opened my mouth to shout a warning but it was too late. What happened next was so fast that I have to slow the action down to describe it to you.

Pierre called to his mother, "Maman, can we go home now?" She turned towards him with her brilliant smile, opened her arms to him, and said, "*Oui, chéri.*" He began to run. The figure in the bushes rose, extended his arm and followed the running boy with what turned out to be a navy Colt. That was when I shouted, but my cry was drowned by a much louder noise.

The boy reached his mother and passed into her embrace. But to avoid being knocked off her feet by his weight, she swept him into her arms and turned, as a parent will do. My shout of warning and the crash of the Colt came together. I saw the lovely young woman shudder as if she had been punched in the back, which in fact she had, for, in turning, she had stopped the bullet intended for her son.

The man in the mask whirled towards the gunshot, saw the figure amid the bushes, pulled something from beneath his cloak, extended his arm and fired. I heard the crack of the tiny Derringer with its single bullet, but one was enough. Ten yards from me the assassin threw both hands to his face. When he fell he crashed out of the bushes onto the snow and lay face upwards in the frosty dawn, a single hole showing black in the center of his forehead.

I was rooted to my spot behind the hedge. I could not move. I thank Providence there was nothing I could do anyway. What I could have done earlier, I was too late to do now, for I had seen and heard so much and understood so little.

At the second gunshot the boy, still uncomprehending, released his mother, who sank to her knees. There was a red stain already spreading on her back. The soft leaden slug had not penetrated her to hit the son in her arms, but had remained inside her. The vicomte gave a cry of "Christine" and ran forward to take her in his arms. She leaned back in his embrace, looked up at him and smiled.

Father Kilfoyle was on his knees in the snow beside her. He ripped off the broad sash around his waist, kissed both ends of it and draped it around his neck. He was praying rapidly and urgently, tears streaming down his rugged Irish face. The man in the mask dropped his small pistol in the snow and stood like a statue, head bowed. His shoulders heaved silently as he wept.

The boy Pierre alone seemed at first unable to take in what had happened. One second his mother was embracing him, the next she was dying in front of his eyes. The first time he called "Maman" it was like a question. The second and third time, like a piteous cry. Then, as if seeking explanation, he turned to the vi-comte. "Papa?" he asked.

Christine de Chagny opened her eyes and her gaze found Pierre. She spoke for the last time, quite clearly, before that divine voice was silenced forever. She said, "Pierre, this is not really Papa. He has brought you up as his own, but your true father is there." She nodded towards the bowed figure in the mask. "I am sorry, my darling."

Then she died. I will not make a big production out of it. She just died. Her eyes closed, the last breath rattled out of her and her head tilted sideways onto the chest of her husband. There was complete silence for several seconds, which seemed like an age. The boy looked from one man to the other. Then he asked of the vicomte once more, "Papa?"

Now, over the past few days I had come to think of the French aristocrat as a kind and decent man but somewhat ineffectual, compared, say, to the dynamic priest. But now something seemed to come into him.

The body of his dead wife lay cradled in the crook

of his left arm. With his right hand he sought one of hers and slowly removed from it a golden ring. I recalled the closing scene at the opera, when the soldier with the shattered face had given her back that very ring as a sign that he accepted their love could never be. The French vicomte took the ring from her finger and pressed it into the palm of his devastated stepson.

A yard away Father Kilfoyle remained on his knees. He had given the diva final absolution before death and, his duty done, he prayed for her immortal soul.

Vicomte de Chagny scooped his dead wife up in his arms and rose to his feet. Then the man who had brought up another's son as his own spoke in his halting English.

"It is true, Pierre. Maman was right. I have done everything for you that I could, but I was never your natural father. The ring belongs to him, who is your father in God's eyes. Give it back to him. He loved her too, and in a way I never could.

"I am going to take the only woman I ever loved back to lie in the soil of France. Today, here, this hour, you have ceased to be a boy and become a man. Now you must make your own choice."

He stood there, his wife in his arms, waiting for an answer. Pierre turned and stared long at the figure of the man identified as his blood father.

The man I had come to call simply the Phantom of Manhattan stood alone with his head bowed, the very distance that separated him from the others seeming to represent the distance to which the human race had pushed him. The hermit, the eternal outsider who had once thought that he had some chance of acceptance into human joys and had been rebuffed. Now every line of his body told me he had once lost everything he ever cared for and was going to lose it all again.

There was silence for several seconds as the boy stared across the clearing. In front of me was what the French call a *tableau vivant*. Six figures, two of them dead and four in pain.

The French vicomte was on one knee cradling the torso of his dead wife. He had laid his cheek on the top of her head which lolled against his chest, stroking the dark hair as if to comfort her.

The Phantom stood motionless, head still bowed, utterly defeated. Darius lay a few feet from me, open-eyed, staring up at a winter sky he could no longer see. The boy stood next to his stepfather, everything he had ever believed in and held to be the immutable order now torn to pieces in violence and bewilderment.

The priest was still on his knees, face turned upwards, eyes closed, but I noticed the big hard hands clutching his metal cross and the lips moving in silent prayer. Later, still consumed by my own inability to explain what happened next, I visited him at his home in the slums of the Lower East Side. What he told me I still do not really understand, but I relate it to you.

He said that in that noiseless clearing he could hear silent screams. He could hear the keening grief of the quiet Frenchman a few feet away. He could hear the bewildered pain of the boy whom he had tutored for seven years. But over all this, he said, he could hear something else. There was in that clearing a lost soul, crying in agony like Coleridge's wandering albatross, planing alone through a sky of pain above an ocean of despair. He was praying that this lost soul might find safe haven in the love of God again. He was praying for a miracle which could not possibly happen. Look, I was a brash Jewish kid from the Bronx. What did I know of lost souls, redemption and miracles? I can only tell you what I saw.

Pierre slowly walked across the clearing towards him. He lifted a hand and removed the wide-brimmed hat. I thought the man in the mask uttered a low whimper. For the skull was bald, save for a few tufts of sparse hair, and the skin was blotched with livid scars and ribbed like molten wax. Without a word the boy eased away the mask over the face.

Now, I have seen the bodies on the slabs at Bellevue, some of them many days in the Hudson River; I have seen men killed on the fields of Europe. But I have never seen a face like the one exposed behind the mask. Only a part of the lower jaw on one side, and the eyes from which tears flowed down the ravaged cheeks seemed human in a visage otherwise so disfigured as to remain hardly human. I could at last understand why he wore his mask, and hid himself from mankind and all our society. Yet here he stood, exposed and humiliated in front of us all, and at the hand of a boy who was his own son.

Pierre stared up at the terrible face without visible

shock or revulsion for a long time. Then he dropped the mask from his right hand. He took the left hand of his father and placed the golden ring upon the fourth finger.

Then he reached up with both hands, embraced the weeping man and said quite clearly, "I want to stay here with you, Father."

That's about it, young people. Within hours the story of the assassination of the diva broke over New York. It was put down to a crazed fanatic, himself shot down at the scene of his infamy. It was a version that suited the mayor and the city authorities. As for me, well, it was the one story in my whole career I never wrote up even though I would have been fired if that were known. Too late to write it now.

EPILOGUE

The body of Christine de Chagny was laid to rest beside that of her father in the churchyard of a small village in Brittany from which they both came.

The vicomte, that good and kindly man, retired to his Normandy estates. He never married again and kept a picture of his much-loved wife beside him at all times. He died of natural causes in the spring of 1940 and never lived to see the invasion of his native land.

Father Joe Kilfoyle stayed on and settled in New York, where he founded a refuge and school for the destitute, abused and unwanted children of the Lower East Side. He refused all preferment in the Church, and remained simply Father Joe to generations of underprivileged kids. Throughout, his homes and schools remained remarkably well-endowed but he never revealed where the funds came from. He died, full of years, in the mid-1950s. For his last three years he was confined to a home for old priests in a small town on the coast of Long Island where the nuns who looked after him reported that he would sit on the open deck, wrapped in a blanket, staring eastwards across the sea and dreaming of a farm near Mullingar.

Oscar Hammerstein later lost control of the Manhattan Opera to the Met, which drove it out of business. His grandson, Oscar III, collaborated with Richard Rodgers to write musicals in the 1950s.

Pierre de Chagny completed his schooling in New York, graduated from an Ivy League university and joined his father at the head of the enormous family corporation. During the First World War both men changed the family name from Muhlheim to another, still widely known and respected in America to this day.

The corporation became famous for its philanthropy across a wide range of social issues, founded a major institution for the correction of disfigurement and created many charitable foundations.

The father retired in the early twenties to a secluded property in Connecticut where he lived out his days with books, paintings and his beloved music. He was attended by two war veterans, each cruelly

EPILOGUE

disfigured while fighting in the trenches, and after that day in Battery Park never wore his mask again.

The son, Pierre, married once and died of old age in the year the first American landed on the moon. His four children live on.

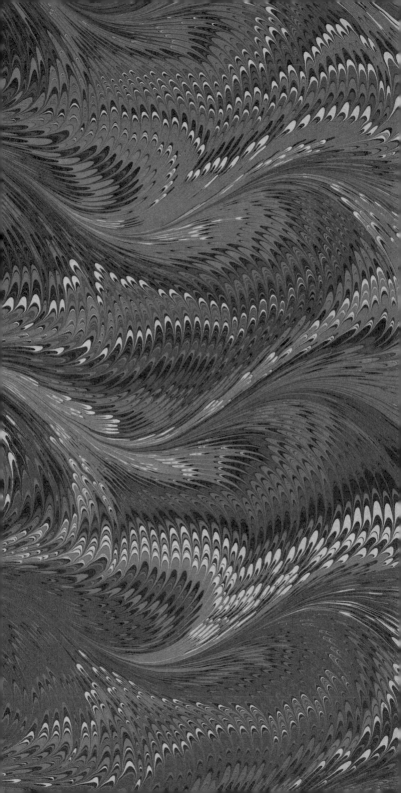